CW00400580

Special Te

A Gay Coming-Out Romance

By Angus MacGregor

©X2Books 2016

1. The Letter

The young man's hands shook as he reread the letter. How could such an innocuous piece of paper change your life so easily, he thought? He felt the smile creep across his face as he took in the message the mail had delivered: he had just landed a football scholarship, a full scholarship to Western Oregon University. All the long hours of practice, the injuries, the early morning runs, the weights...it had all paid off. He was heading to the Wolf Pack as a freshman punter. He thought his heart would burst it was pounding so hard.

His dad had been patiently waiting for him to react, to let him know what the letter had contained. As the blond haired teenager looked up with tears shimmering in his eyes, the small, stocky man looked petrified.

"So what does it say, son?"

"I got in. I made it, Dad. Full ride to WOU."

The father shouted and wrapped his boy in an iron bear hug that threatened to break the boy's ribs. The boy's father rained down kisses on the side of his face and even planted one mighty fat kiss on his thick lips, pressing his scratchy mustache tightly against his son's mouth. The men jumped up and down like rabbits, shouting and crying for joy. Paul Phillips had been there for his boy every step of the way and he was so proud, he was ready to explode.

Paul stood back and held his son at arm's length, just drinking it all in and appreciating the man he had become. Dakota was a good size boy, 6-2, lean frame but big strong thighs and legs that could boot a ball halfway to Klamath Falls. His blond curls were tamed by the tight high haircut that made him look about the same as he had when he was three. His impossibly big green eyes sparkled with happiness. The soft blond mustache and chin whiskers did little to age him. He had always been this cute, furry kid. Even when he was five, a fine downy layer of blond fuzz shone on his arms and legs. The kid matured early too, sporting a big penis, heavy sack, and pubic hair in the fifth grade, almost two years earlier than many of the other boys. Paul recalled taking Dakota to the pool with some other boys his age and the other boys careful stares as the boy dried off and moved around the locker room with confidence in his looks. The other boys kept their towels close around their hairless crotches for the most part, but spent plenty of time checking out Dakota and Paul, for that matter. Paul never mentioned it but he could tell the boy enjoyed the stares at his impressive dick and balls. He had stood with his son under the hair dryers naked, enjoying the stares and appreciative grins from the other boys. Little by little, more of them would join in the fun, hanging out naked in the locker room, enjoying being men and boys joined together in the ritual of male bonding.

Paul's wife had left him when Dakota was fourteen, having found a younger man at work that was better at fucking her and putting up with her bullshit than Paul had been. She had moved away to Seattle and Dakota began to spend less and less time with her. She ended up getting pregnant again, this time with a daughter, and more or less forgot about her almost grown son. The men had grown close, Paul wondered if sometimes they were too close. He hadn't had a date for more than four years. He knew he shouldn't be so emotionally connected with his boy, but they had worked out a relationship that worked for them both. Dakota loved football like a koala loves eucalyptus leaves. Paul had secretly been relieved when his boy showed little interest in dating or losing his shit over some little high school beauty. He had gone out a few times for big events, like prom. But most of his waking hours were spent either practicing or watching film or figuring out how to become a better athlete. Many times, the men would lay on Paul's bed watching a game or some television show, only to fall asleep and spend the night curled up together. Secretly, it was the most comforting thing he could imagine and he wondered how in the hell he was supposed to watch his boy head off to college and not get depressed and lonely. Maybe it would be time to get back on the dating wagon, he wondered. Like a lot of other men his age, Paul masturbated practically every day, and he found that for the most part, it satisfied his libido. From the smell of the boy's room, the pile of used socks, underwear, and damp cum rags, he knew Dakota had no problem taking care of his teen boy sexual urges. He knew it was weird, but on several occasions, he had pressed the used rags, underwear, and socks to his nose as he jerked off, adding his own load to his boy's laundry. He never fantasized about having sex with his son, it was more than he got off on watching him turn into a man and imagining the fun he was going to have with his own sexual development. The feel of sliding his cock into his boy's dirty shorts and unloading a fat blast of nut into the soft cotton that had been cradling his son's boys was a pervy turn on that he kept to himself.

"Wow, just like that...your life kind of changes in a huge way," Paul said.

"I can hardly believe it. It's going to be so weird moving away and all."

Paul ruffled his short blond curls. His love for this boy was overwhelming, as was his pride in his abilities, work ethic, and yeah, his good looks. "It will be great for you," he said, already feeling the lonesomeness in his heart.

"At least it's just a couple of hours away. Not like getting an offer from Penn State."

"That would have been a bit hard for me."

"Me too, although I was really curious about seeing the Sandusky shower room."

"You are a bad boy," Paul said with a fake spank to his son's round ass.

"Yeah, I probably would have been one of his special boys."

Paul looked at Dakota and smirked. "There would be no doubt about that, kiddo. So when do you show up and start training with the team?"

"Looks like there are a few opportunities in the spring to go in for conditioning and OTA stuff, then report to school around the first of August. Shit, I wonder who I will get for a roommate? Hopefully, not some weirdo."

"I think you're gonna do just fine. They will all be your teammates. You are easy to get along with, bubba. They will let you know soon so you can get in touch with him, though."

Dakota looked at his dad with deep gratitude and gratefulness. "I couldn't have done this without you, Dad. You mean everything to me," the boy said hugging his father hard once again. Paul felt tears prick at the corners of his eye.

"Hey kiddo, it's always been your big heart that made this happen. I just was along for the ride."

2 – Dad's Graduation Gift

Dakota looked around the outside of the dorm, breathing deeply. The warm Oregon sun was already high in the sky. August can be as hot in the Northwest as it is Texas sometimes. The tall player wore a new WOU tank top and black shorts. He held his hand up, shielding the sun from his eyes as he tried to size up the dorm and figure out where he was. The breeze ruffled the thick blond fur under his armpits. He instantly liked the little college town of Monmouth, finding its size and easy of moving around a welcome relief from Medford. He found the front door to the dorm and made his way to the housing window. A pretty brunette girl with nice round tits and a small ring in her left nostril smiled brightly.

"Hey, welcome to WOU. What's your name?"

"Dakota Phillips."

"Let's see...oh here you are. Punter, huh? Cool. Looks like you are in 425. Let's see if they have a roommate assigned to you yet?"

"I got a note saying it was a dude with last name McLeod...first initial B."

"Oh yeah. Here it is. His name is Bear McLeod."

"Bear, huh?"

"Yep." She snickered. "Cool name for a football player. Looks like he is hmmm, LS. What's that?"

"Probably long snapper. Guess they put the special teams boys together," Dakota said.

The girl continued to snicker and make silly eyes at Dakota, licking her lips over and over.

"Are your lips chapped?" he asked knowing they were not. But sometimes, he really enjoyed being a dick. "I've got some Chapstick." He offered the tube."

"Eww, I don't even know you," she said acting as if he had offered her a quick taste of his cock. He took his key and access card and said good morning and left to find his room. He turned around and asked. "Any idea when Bear is showing up?"

The girl looked confused and annoyed now. But she clacked on a keyboard and said in a snappy voice, "Looks like not until tomorrow."

"Okay. Thanks a lot."

"Whatever," Miss Congeniality said.

Dakota ran up the stairs and found his room close to the end of the hall. He went inside to size up the place. It looked like a million other dorm rooms, except that the room was laid out with the beds almost touching, a fake wall divider between them that only stuck up less than a foot, meaning that you were practically in the bed with your roommate. Dakota frowned. He knew he was going to lose his privacy sharing a room, but he was surprised he was practically going to be sharing a bed too.

"Fuck, I hope you aren't a snoring Bear, Bear," he muttered to himself.

He did like the way his desk and other furniture created his own side to the room and in the end, thought it was a pretty good setup. And he was positively giddy about the fact they had their own small bathroom attached to the room with a toilet and walk-in shower. The sink was out in the main room along with a small fridge. Dakota felt his belly rumble and closed the door to the bathroom.

"Might as well christen the shitter," he said aloud. He pulled his phone out so he could relax like every other guy in the world these days. He slid open the phone and scrolled across a couple of pages, finding a small folder and opened it up. Buried several levels deep, he accessed the Grindr app and opened it. He looked at the photos of guys on the app, noticing that several were just 1000 ft away or so. He was surprised how many put up their faces, something he had never been able to do. His profile photo was his flexed bicep, with a close-up of his furry armpit. He opened several profiles, most not that interesting. The fact was, Dakota had been on the app for over a year, but so far, he had never met up with a guy from here.

The handsome athlete had been working out exactly how he felt about sex and sexuality and all of that for the better part of three years. Like every other guy, he spent a ton of time watching porn vids and found that a lot of them got his rocks off. He liked watching guys bang girls, he liked watching guys bang other guys too. He tried out masturbation vids, sex toy vids, hardcore shit like watersports and simulated forced sex. He even looked at some dad-son role play sites and had to admit, he had jizzed a river of nut watching them. In fact, the only vids he really didn't spend any time with were the girl on girl ones. He just didn't see the point. He liked imagining himself in the story and all those wet pussies, long pink nails, high heels and fake boobs just didn't do it for him. He knew he was in the small minority of guys who didn't get moist watching two chicks munch on each other, but he honestly just found it boring.

His phone buzzed and he saw he got a message on the app.

+Dude, show your face and cock.

Dakota rolled his eyes. +Maybe later he answered. The guy who had sent the message was quite femmy looking with several strange notes in his bio like "nipple clips and fisting." Yikes. Dakota blocked the guy and shook his head. He relaxed and sent a massive turd into the toilet with a loud kerplunk. *God, is there anything better than the first shit of the morning*, he wondered.

He spent the rest of the morning unloading his car. He put away his clothes, made up his bed, deciding on the one on the right-hand side of the room. He put up a few posters and some Christmas lights, hoping that was still cool to do and not total loser. At the end, he stood back and felt pretty good about the way his side of the room looked. He wondered if Bear was going to be a slob or a neat freak like him. With a name like Bear...he was prepared for an Odd Couple sort of dynamic. But he liked messy big guys and figured it would probably all work out.

He walked down the street and grabbed a ridiculously huge burrito at Coyote's. He couldn't even finish it. It was a little greasy, but all in all, really tasty and only $4. Damn. It was about 2:30 and now that he was full, he was sleepy as well and as usual, a little horny too. He bent down and pulled out a box from underneath his bed and opened it up. He had gotten a number of great graduation gifts but this one from his dad, though outrageous, was one of his faves. He picked up the note and instantly felt homesick. He read.

Hey D,

I know this is the craziest thing in the world for me to give you, but WTF. You and I have very few secrets and in the past couple of years are practically an old married couple around the house with each other. I just want to say once again how proud I am of you. Every day, my heart just swells to bursting with gratitude for you and the wonderful relationship we have. Thanks for being the best son a dad could ever hope for.

I know you will find friends and hopefully, maybe even a really GOOD friend. Hope your school and sports will always been your priority...at least for now. Shoot for the stars buddy.

Hope you aren't totally creeped out by the gift. Shit, I got one of these for myself. I'm thinking about giving him a name. LOL. Happy times.

Dad

Nestled in the tissue paper was a brand new Fleshlight. The audacity of his dad giving him a masturbation toy was just a perfect testimony to the close relationship they had. His dad had always been up front with him about sex, explaining everything when he was young. He had walked him through the funny avenues of puberty, allaying his fears about being a freak, and letting him know that jacking off wasn't only normal, it was fucking healthy as well. He had taken his dad at his word and established himself as a world-class masturbator, normally rubbing one off twice a day. His dad had walked in on him spanking it at least a dozen times. At first he was embarrassed, then it became a joke. Finally, it was almost some sort of strange turn on to have his dad crash his private time. And shit, he had walked in on his dad almost as much. And goddamn, his dad stroked his pole as much as anyone. More than once, he had stood back and watched the big explosion of sperm jet from his dad's mighty erection, splattering all over his hairy belly and chest, only to head back to his room and do the same himself. The idea his dad was sliding his big cock into one of these contraptions back home was actually a huge turn on, not a gross out.

Dakota picked up the smooth handle and studied the opening of the device. It had changeable openings: a mouth, a pussy, or an asshole. He took off the pussy attachment and fitted the mouth onto the handle. He lifted his round ass off the bed and pulled off his shorts and underwear. His dick was already more than half hard. He stroked a few times, loving the feeling of his shaft filling with blood and standing up straight. His penis rose like a rocket from his tidy honey-colored bush. The large mushroom head was dark pink and oozed a small trail of precum. He rubbed the fluid around the wide head and licked his finger. He brought out the bottle of Gun Oil his dad had also provided (He had gotten a new bottle of lube about every three months from his father.) He tipped up the bottle, luxuriating in the feel of the slick juice running down his shaft to his large, smooth balls. He stroked his penis, smiling as it glistened in the sun coming through his window. He picked up the Fleshlight and laid the opening against his cock and penetrated the lips with his erection. His eyes automatically closed as the tight sleeve gripped his penis like a tight glove. He buried his dick deep into the toy, until it rested against his pubes, then slid it up almost to the end and then drove it back down.

"Fuck that feels amazing," Dakota whispered to himself. He closed his eyes and concentrated on the grip the toy had on his cock. It was tight and slid so easily, sucking his penis deep into the handle. He moved the thing back and forth until the room filled with the squish-squash of the tube manipulating his Johnson. He spread his legs wide, his balls hanging down low. His left hand was still slick with the Gun Oil. He felt between his legs, under his sack and found his asshole and gasped as he penetrated the tightness knuckle deep. He was lost in a reverie of sex and passion. Images filled his mind: that beautiful girl from the Quantico TV show, his senior English lit teacher, Rob Gronkowski, Chris Pratt...oh God, Chris Pratt, sucking my dick. Sliding his big fingers into my boyhole. Dakota felt his climax build in his balls and bubble up like a fire hose and explode into the gripping sleeve of the Fleshlight. The toes on his big size 13 feet curled and he dumped gush after gush of hot gravy into the slurping mouth of the toy.

Exhausted, he lay back on the pillow, the toy still rigid on his cock, bobbing back and forth on his mighty erection.

"Thanks, Dad. That's the best graduation present ever," he whispered.

"You can fucking say that again," a low voice rumbled from the doorway.

Dakota's eyes flew open.

3 – The New Roommate

Dakota sat up in bed like he was launched from a giant toaster, his hard cock still buried deep inside the infernal Fleshlight. A large, hairy young man stood inside the room, his mouth wide open, staring like a laser at the naked athlete on the bed attached to the sex toy. He stupidly grabbed his pillow and slammed it over his crotch, his face burning hot and red like lava.

"Motherfucker!" he hissed, his face a mixture of anger and mortification. "What the hell, man?"

The young man finally tore his gaze away from Dakota's impressive performance and looked at the blond punter, bemused, but decidedly apologetic as well.

"Ah bro. I had no idea you were in here or that you were…um, busy. I got into town way early. So I just came up to unload. Fuck man, I am really sorry." The big boy took a tentative step closer and extended a large hand toward Dakota.

Dakota stared at the hand in utter bewilderment, but released the handle of the Fleshlight and nervously held out his own. He shook the boy's hand, watching the kid have dawning realization sweep over his face. As he pulled his hand back, he looked at his palm and then back at Dakota. There was a long, pregnant pause before both of them exploded in hysterics.

The boys lay on Dakota's bed, laughter shaking the mattress and reverberating around the room. Dakota was embarrassed beyond words, but this giant's musical laugh and unassuming personality helped him not want to simply die. He leaned up on one elbow, his feet pressed against the legs of the student at the bottom of his bed. He held the pillow tight over his middle, but finally figured, what the hell. He tossed it and the Fleshlight to the floor and pulled his underwear back over his now clearly deflated penis and sat up, looking inquisitively at the furry boy wiping tears from his eyes. He rolled over and actually patted Dakota on the knee and smiled.

"Man, I mean it, I am really sorry for barging in on you and your, um...buddy there." He sputtered and both athletes broke into a new chorus of laughter.

"Well either you are the worst peeping Tom in history, or I suppose you are my roommate," Dakota said.

"That I am. Bear McLeod, long snapper," the student's bright blue eyes sparkled, crinkled in mirth at the corners. He held his hand out again, this time shaking Dakota's with all sincerity. "Okay, that was classic. We will tell our grandchildren about that introduction."

"Great...a date that will live in infamy. Let's hope we just have grandsons. I could just seem some sweet little girl's face with that story."

"Oh snap, that's for sure. Well you know what, it's always hard to break the ice in a situation like this. I would say, everything else for us is going to be cake compared to that. And before we leave the elephant, or should I say anaconda, in the corner...Damn, bro. That is some serious junk you got there."

Dakota rolled his eyes and smirked, but he could tell the guys wasn't busting his balls. He was just one of those easy to joke with guys that make you feel at ease even with you have been humiliated. Dakota brazenly reached down and brought the Fleshlight back up into clear view.

"Play your cards right, Bear buddy, and maybe you will get a turn with this baby."

"Jeez. Can I see that? I have seen those online and wondered what it would be like." Dakota handed the plastic toy over to Bear who examined it like an archeologist with a new bone. "Wow, man this thing is kind of cool. Fucking sexy as shit, dude. Hell, it would be fun to take a ride with this guy." With that, he slid his finger into the opening of the mouth. His face contorted and he pulled his finger back out, slick with semen.

"Fuck!" Dakota said humiliated once again.

"Oh shit," Bear said holding his finger up like he had just been poisoned. "Got a hazmat clean up on aisle five!" He said and rolled off the bed to wash his hand at the sink. Dakota picked up the toy and threw it into a nightstand drawer. "Well, don't forget to wash out that bad boy so it's ready to go for round two," he said, still nonchalantly.

"Yeah, that's for sure. Sorry to put you through that, Bear. Welcome to the dorm and your perverted roomie."

The big boy grabbed Dakota and put him in a headlock. It wasn't tight, but there was no way he was going to break out of that. His face was pressed into the player's black armpit fur, ripe and sweaty. "Dude, that ain't nothing I don't do myself a couple of times a day. Shit, me and my brother have spanked it together a dozen times or so. That's what happens when you have a big family and have to share a bedroom your whole life. I never ever had any privacy. My mom just stopped coming up to our room 'cause she was always walking in on one of us all the time. That ever happen to you?"

"Other than this exceptional moment? Um, yeah a few times with my Dad. It's just him and me though, so no big."

"Yeah, for sure. Not like he's not rubbing one off too."

"All the time."

"Sweet. Pretty sure my Dad is a major baloney beater too. I think that's why he built a workshop." Both boys laughed. "So where you from, roomie?"

"Medford. You?"

"Big city of Burns."

"Oh wow, country boy for sure."

Bear leaned back on the counter top. "You know it, but I think I might be slightly more evolved than the normal cretin from the sticks. You have an idea for a major yet?"

"Not really. I love geography. Might just go with that," Dakota said. "You?"

"Probably business or marketing. Hey, you're Dakota, right. Dakota Phillips?"

"Yeah."

"Shit, I know you. You can punt the ball 75 yards sometimes. You're good."

Dakota felt his face flush. "Thanks, bro. I had a great senior year."

"Well, it will be a pleasure to get your between my legs."

"Excuse me?" Dakota said with a shock.

"For the snaps. You know, long snapper? You stare at my big ass and when I hike the ball?"

Dakota laughed. "Oh yeah. That's good. You are huge, so thanks for protecting my ass already."

Bear hopped down and patted Dakota affectionately on his round ass. "Nobody's gonna get to sack this ass with me around...other than me."

"That makes no sense at all."

"Yeah, that's stupid. Sorry."

"So, you want some help bringing in your shit?" Dakota asked pulling on a t-shirt.

"Hey, if you don't mind."

4 – The jog to the park

The players finished bringing in Bear's boxes and clothes in less than thirty minutes. He had less junk than Dakota. Dakota couldn't help but notice that most of Bear's clothes looked well-worn, old, and even second-hand. Most of his stuff was hastily hung up or stashed in closets. He put up a few posters of his own: Game of Thrones, J.J. Watt, and curiously, a poster from the Broadway musical, "Hamilton."

"Wow, you know about this all the way out in Burns?" Dakota asked as the tall boy unfurled the poster and pinned it to the wall.

"Oh you know. There's this magic box thing called a computer and the interwebs...we dumb fucks get to look at shit on there sometimes if we get the chores all done," he said in his most hick voice.

"Har har. I'm serious. There's plenty of city boys who don't know a thing about that show."

"Well then they are stupid because it's awesome."

"I totally agree brother..."Look around, look around..."

Then together both boys sang out…"How lucky we are to be alive right now." Bear grinned widely then stepped close to Dakota. "Acting like that in Burns can get your ass kicked big time."

"Same in Medford, brother."

"Well we can close the door and sing quiet and be a couple of little fags together," Bear said. Then he stopped and looked back at Dakota. "Sorry man, if that was like mean or insensitive or something."

"What the fuck you mean by that? You think I'm gay?"

"What? No, shit. I wasn't trying to…oh damn. I am never going to make it in this politically correct place."

Dakota leaned his arm on Bear's strong shoulder and whispered in his ear…"I am busting your balls, buddy. I love gay shit like musicals. I just keep it to myself."

Bear smiled widely. "Well look at how cos-mo-politan we are. A couple of bohemian hipsters."

"You know it. So, is your name really Bear, or is it short for something."

"What the fuck is bear short for?" the boy asked with a confused grin. "Nah, I was just a big ole kid and my dad named me Bear. My brother is named Big."

"No fuckin' way," Dakota exclaimed.

"Way. And besides, what's up with Dakota? You sound like a man's cologne or a new cigarette or something."

"It's stupid, I know. But….what can you do. Parents are pretty nuts."

"You have no idea, man. My dad is voting for Trump."

"Oh my God!"

"Yeah. Preach it. That Cheet-o face clown can suck my furry hole."

"After he licks my big sack."

*　　*　　*　　*　　*　　*

The guys walked around campus and found most of the landmarks they needed to. They checked in at the athletic complex and met Coach Taylor, the head coach and Coach Johnson, the special teams coach. The whole time they were talking with Coach Johnson, Bear seemed to be on the verge of laughing. He kept coughing to stifle the chuckles, so much so, that the coach offered him a water bottle. As they walked back toward the cafeteria, Dakota asked,

"What's going on with you? Why did you keep choking back there?"

"Did you see the coach's diploma on the wall?" Bear answered.

"No. I mean, I didn't pay any attention. Why?

"Dude, did you check out his name?"

"What? Dakota asked suspiciously.

"His first name is Harry."

"So?"

"Bro!   Harry. Harry Johnson!"

"Oh shit!" The athletes laughed all the way to the cafeteria.

They ate large pita wraps sitting with several other athletes at the table, getting to know a few guys that were either new to the team or returning players. It became apparent in those few moments that some things don't change, namely…if you are on special teams, a certain number of your teammates think you are hardly an important part of the team. No one was rude or dismissive, but it just had that polite sense of acknowledging a clearly inferior person that steamed Dakota. He was in a huff when he and Bear walked back to the dorm.

"What's got you all lit up," Bear said ripping a loud belch in the process.

"Wow, there's no end to your talents." Dakota snapped.

"Hey now, don't be a douche. What's got your nuts all in a twist?"

Dakota kicked a fir cone that had fallen to the sidewalk. "It just burns my butter when I hear DBs or RBs or anyone on the team downplay special teams players, like we are the remedial class of the football team. I mean, they can't fucking play without us. We make and break teams all the time. I mean, show some respect!" Dakota fumed.

Bear smiled and wrapped a big, heavy arm around Dakota's neck in a fatherly gesture. His thick, furry pits were fragrant with the slightest hint of sweat and man stank that for some reason, caused Dakota's dick to swell.

"Bubba, it's always like that. Special Teams be like the janitorial crew of the team. No one gives us much love, but they be fucked without us. Don't worry about it. In fact, my old man used to tell me: 'Boy, you best make sure no one on the team hardly remembers your name 'cause you do your job so well. "Cause believe you me, if you fuck up, then they will remember you and it will always be bad.'"

Dakota laughed. "Thanks, Pop," he said elbowing Bear softly in the ribs. The big man pulled Dakota's head toward him and ruffled his short, blond curls.

"That's my boy," Bear said. "Hey, you feel like a run after dinner? Just feel kind of all stiff and don't want to be all tight tomorrow for first practice."

"Sure. Guess we can check out more of the town that way," Dakota said.

Ten minutes later, the players jogged along the main avenue leading out of the campus toward the south part of town. They wore tank tops and lose shorts, enjoying the late afternoon sun as they ran along the sidewalks and then, moved into the road as they jogged on Warren Street toward the south.

"This little town is pretty cute," Dakota said. "At least there are a bunch of cool restaurants and all."

"Shit, this place is like big time compared to my town. Fine dining in Burns is going to the A&W or the Indian Casino for steak and lobster night."

They ran past a hillside cemetery and then on Haltom Road alongside the Calapooia River. The air was still and filled with the buzz or chirp of bugs or birds and the steady padding of their running shoes. Dakota loved the feeling of his legs warming up and his balls slowing bouncing in his jock as he ran alongside Bear. There was something intrinsically comforting hanging out with this big goob, he thought, and was privately grateful his roommate hadn't been one of the teammates that seemed marginally disrespectful at dinner. He liked listening to Bear's down-home banter and easy-going style. He knew he burned too hot most of the time and needed to chill out. It was way easier when he was around a level-headed guy like Bear. Dakota looked ahead and saw a bridge over the river and a sign to a park.

"Hey, let's go into the park and check it out. I think they have trails and shit that go down to the river."

"Lead the way, Lewis and Clark," Bear huffed.

The college students jogged down the drive into the park and moved around the pavement that encircled the forested wayside. There were two vehicles in the park but all the picnic tables were empty. They made their way halfway around the circle, checking out the view of the river and the various trails that headed down toward the water.

"Hey brother, I gotta drain the weasel," Bear said, nodding his head toward a park bathroom.

"Yeah, my iced tea is calling," Dakota said. They slowed and entered the bathroom. It was a typical rural park restroom, dark, depressing, and rank. It was clean with no trash or obvious nastiness around, but it still smelled like an old pit toilet for all intents and purposes. Bear walked up to the urinal and Dakota went around the wall into the stall. He pulled out his dick and exhaled, watching the yellow bubbles in the toilet bowl as he pissed. He could hear Bear beside him peeing loudly and ripping an echoing fart into the quiet of the bathroom.

"Charming, bro," Dakota said listening to Bear giggle.

"Better out than in," he said rolling off another loud, protracted blast.

"Jesus, man."

"Hey, what's this?" Bear said.

Dakota looked down and saw the young man's fingers wiggling through a smooth round hole in the plywood stall wall. There were obvious white stains around the sickly green paint on the wood.

"Dude, I wouldn't touch that if I were you."

"How come? By the way, you have a nice dick, bro."

Dakota looked over and saw Bear's eye and smile in the hole. He turned his penis toward the hole like he was going to pee into it. Bear yelped and leaned back. "So why's this hole here? Shouldn't they plug it up?"

Dakota shook his head and smiled, pushing his penis back into his jock and shorts. "It's a fucking glory hole, man. You know?"

"Glory what? I don't know what that is."

Dakota bent down and looked through the hole with Bear doing the same on the other side. "A glory hole. You stick your dick through it so the guy on the other side gives you a beejur, but it's more anonymous."

"Guys don't do that," Bear answered.

"I promise you they do."

"You mean like this?" Bear said and with that, his massive penis slid through the hole, half hard, along with his egg-sized balls.

"Yaaah! You almost took out my eye, man. Yeah, just like that. Guys suck each other off like that."

"No fuckin' way," Bear said waggling his penis back and forth. "Damn, I don't know anything," he said. He pulled his pecker of the hole and back into his shorts. He turned and washed his hands in the sink with Dakota using the sink beside him.

"Bro, there's plenty of guys who don't know much about that. I just happened to have seen it before."

"Who told you about that shit?"

"Actually, my dad."

Bear laughed. "My old man would shit before he would ever tell me anything like that, not that he would know about it anyway. Wow, I am such a country bumpkin. Glory Hole...who the hell does that?"

"Lots of guys from what I understand. But it's pretty gross,"

"Yeah, did you see all the cum stains. Ewww."

"I know. Let's get out of here before someone wants us to blow them," Dakota said with a chuckle.

The guys jogged into the nearest trail opening and down the path toward the river. It was thick overgrown brambles and hedges on either side most of the way, with the occasional side trail that went off somewhere. They slowed to a walk and moved along the path, stopping to watch the sunset sparkle on the slow moving water. As they stood still, a strange sound quietly reverberated from nearby. The guys listened and turned their heads toward the sound. Bear stretched his neck, his eyes growing wide as he clearly spied something. He put a finger to his lips and motioned for Dakota to follow him. The guys moved quietly into the undergrown, pulling vines out of the way, stopping behind a massive maple tree. Dakota gasped and pulled back into the shadows.

In front of them, two shirtless men embraced, running their hands over one another's chest and belly. One of the men was older, with mostly silver hair, a deep tan, greying chest hair and a trim goatee. The other man was younger, maybe a college student. He was smooth, lean, muscled, and hugely erect. His long, think penis was rock hard and shaved. The dad dropped to his knees and took the young man's cock into his mouth and sucked him skillfully, gripping his smooth ass as he did so. The boy gripped the man's head and face fucked him deeply, his balls slapping against the man's chin.

After a few moments, the older man stood up and pushed the college boy to his knees. The man pulled out a thick cock encircled by a chrome cock ring that held his beer can sized penis and bull balls. The young man opened his mouth and took the dad's cock balls deep into his mouth, pulling the man's ass further and further to get more of his cock in his hungry mouth. The man's head was thrown back as he pushed in and out of the boy's mouth, his heavy balls mashing into the young man's tiny chin whiskers. Soon, the young man stood up and turned around, presenting his ass to the silver bear who dropped to his knees and fastened his mouth on the young man's asshole like a starving wolf. The college boy held on to a small sapling as the dad licked and ate his asshole until it ran wet with saliva. The bear stood again and smacked his erection against the young man's crack and manipulated his penis to rest against the guy's hole. He grunted and pushed forward, sliding roughly inside the boy. The young man groaned, bending down low, rocking back and forth as the man plowed him deep and hard, his belly smacking sharply against the student's smooth ass. The silver bear fucked fast and deep, sweat pouring from his face, as he gripped the boy's shoulders breeding him with all the power he could muster.

With a loud grunt, the man ejaculated into the young man's ass, sending load after load into his stretched pussy. The man lay against the boy briefly then pulled out. The young man's asshole gaped wide open and a gush of white semen flowed out onto the leaf-strewn path. Bear's hand gripped Dakota's arm and the two quietly retreated back to the path and then to the pavement. Wordlessly, they jogged away, looking back over their shoulders to see if the men emerged. A few minutes later, Bear spoke.

"Holy shit! I have never seen anything like that before. Fuck me, dude. Do guys bone each other like that all the time? Jesus!"

"I haven't seen that before either, I mean, other than maybe online shit."

"I ain't ever even seen that on the internet. I mean, I guess I knew it was out there, but I just never...holy shit!"

Dakota snickered. "Got you pretty turned on though, didn't it?" Dakota reached over and gently let his hand brush against the obvious erection bouncing in Bear's shorts.

"Hell yeah. I mean, who could watch that and not get boned up?"

"Well not me. I'm running fully loaded here too. It's about to kill me. Feels like my junk is ready to break off."

"Word, bro," Bear said holding his balls as they jogged back to the dorm.

5 – The First Night

Dakota and Bear jogged back to the dorm at a fast clip. Both athletes were gasping and sweating by the time they made their way back up the elevator to their room. Sweat poured down their faces, arms and legs, plastering their hair against their head and shirts to their backs. Dakota walked to the mini fridge and pulled out two bottles of water and handed one to Bear who downed it in one long gulp. They stood in the middle of the room, not wanting to sit on their furniture or beds due to the sweat. Bear pulled off his shirt and used it to wipe down his back. Dakota watched the muscles on his strong back ripple and flow under the movement of the shirt. Soft brown hairs covered the small of Bear's back, making a triangle of fur right above his ass crack. The top of his shoulders was covered with plastered fur.

"You want to shower first?" Dakota asked pulling off his own shirt and wiping himself down. He saw Bear's gaze on him as well.

"Nah. I'm still too winded. You go first."

Dakota rummaged around in his drawers for some new underwear. He thought about it for a moment, but in the end, decided to slide his wet shorts and underwear off out in the room and toss into his dirty clothes hamper. He picked up a towel and walked naked into the bathroom, feeling Bear's eyes on him the whole time. He turned on the water and stepped into the shower, the cool water sliding over his body like a balm. He lathered up his pits and chest, before moving to his balls and ass crack. His mind filled with images from the park as he washed, his dick growing harder by the minute. He soaped up his furry crack and slid his middle finger up inside his ass, probing himself deep and hard, stroking his cock as he did so. All he could think of was the young man submitting his tender ass to the silver dad, holding tight, while the man bred him like a bull. He shoved another finger up inside his ass and then added another. Now, in his mind, he was bent over holding the tree. As he looked behind him, he saw Bear's kind face, mouth open in a silent O, his large hands gripping his shoulders plowing himself as far inside Dakota's ass as possible. With a gasp, Dakota's orgasm exploded, shooting three large blasts of semen against the shower wall and over his hand. Dakota leaned back against the cool tile and looked at the white streaks of sperm on his fingers. He closed his eyes and slid his fingers into his mouth, tasting the sour, salty fluid on his tongue. He finished soaping up and rinsing off. He turned off the shower and dried off his arms, back, and legs before stepping out. He almost shouted when he did.

"Oh sorry, roomie. I was having a bit of a crisis there. Was gonna be a photo finish if I didn't drop a load," Bear said looking up from the toilet. He sat naked, with his legs spread wide, his penis hard and erect between his legs. His large, strong chest was covered in black fur across his pecs and down the middle of his belly to his navel, spreading into a wide V around his crotch. His legs were carpeted with fur down to his toes. The air in the small bathroom was thick with steam and sweat and shit. "Sorry about the smell, bro."

Dakota smiled. This was new for sure. He had almost never taken a shit in his entire life with someone else around since he was about thirteen. There were those rare occasions when he and his dad had taken a dump while the other was in the shower or shaving or what not, but it was unusual. Here in this tiny room, Bear filled up the space with his huge body, his sweat, and stink, but for some reason, it wasn't off-putting. Dakota reached out and patted his roommate on the head, his naked cock hovering inches in front of the young man's face. Bear looked up and pulled his face back.

"Woah, brother. I think I'll pass on the sausage sandwich right now. I think I've had enough up-close time with another man's D today."

Dakota noticed Bear didn't take his gaze off his penis the whole time he was complaining. Dakota wrapped the towel around his middle and started to work on his hair in front of the mirror. Bear closed his phone and wiped up and flushed. He took up so much room in the tiny bathroom, it seemed impossible. He turned on the shower and climbed in. In a moment, he was singing and washing in a loud, animated voice.

"I saw two dude butt fuck in the woods..." he sang the made-up song like a contestant on The Voice. Suddenly, his song stopped and his head came out of the shower.

"Holy shit, roomie. You left your big splooge all over the shower wall. I just wiped some of it off with my Johnson by accident!"

Dakota hooted hysterically as Bear threw the bar of soap at his head, barely missing him.

Dakota was sitting at his computer reading some Reddit feeds and checking Facebook when Bear came out of the bathroom. He was drying his hair with his towel, the rest of him happy and naked. Dakota indulged himself and stared thoughtfully at the young man's cock that was full and thick, resting on one of the biggest nutsacks Dakota had ever seen. The guy's penis was mesmerizing for some reason and he felt like the world's biggest homosexual for wanting to go over and just hold it for a moment to examine it closely. *What the fuck is wrong with me*, he thought. *I am going gaga over my roommate, some big furry goob from Eastern Oregon like it was a Sports Illustrated swimsuit model. But then, the thought to himself, when was the last time he cared about pretty girls*? He looked up and Bear was staring back at him with a crooked smile on his face.

"You checking out my sack, Bucko?" Bear said reaching down and wiggling his massive testicles.

"What? Oh, hell no. I was just...um.."

"Lost in thought?"

"Yeah," Dakota said.

"Lost in thought about how much you want to hold my pecker?"

"You are a sick puppy," Dakota said flipping him the finger.

"Here now, I must be hitting a nerve," Bear said walking over closer to Dakota whose back was to him at his desk, "Cause you are resorting to abuse."

"Who the hell are you?" Dakota said laughing. "You sound like my Dad or something." Dakota felt a warm softness on his shoulder and looked over. Resting on his bare shoulder was Bear's heavy nutsack and penis. Dakota yelped and pulled away.

"Jesus Christ!"

"No, just good ole Bear McLeod," the big man said with his hands on his hips, a wide grin spreading across his face. "Man, you should have seen your face. My bro back home and me, we are always pulling that shit on each other and even my old man."

"You lay your dick on your Dad's shoulder?" Dakota asked incredulously.

"Yeah, if he's being a real prick or something. Man, he hollers big time but I think down deep, he thinks it's pretty funny. Fuck, he's the one that did it to us first."

Dakota laughed. "Okay, that is pretty funny…and totally twisted too. My Dad is crazy too but he's never laid his meat on my shoulder for a joke. Don't you want to get dressed, buddy? I mean, are you just gonna be naked the whole time we live together?"

"Well not the whole time, but yeah, I'm kind of a let it all hang out guy, especially when there are no girls around. You don't mind do you?" Bear waited until Dakota was watching and deliberately bent over to dry his feet exposing his furry crack and asshole to his roommate."

"Yaah, my eyes. Some things can't be unseen, dude." Bear exploded with laughter.

The guys settled down and spent the next hour filling our online forms for classes and looking at class schedules. Bear mercifully slid on a pair of shorts to cover his wide backside, but Dakota got the idea, living with him was always going to be an exercise in patience. But the big goof was so likeable and kind, you just couldn't get too mad. And if he was honest, he actually liked the big ox strutting around in all his furry naked glory. He loved watching his muscles and strong arms and legs gracefully move around, the opposite of what you would expect a big man like him to be like. The guys chatted back and forth, discussing football teams they admired, television shows, and favorite foods. A knock at the door broke the conversation and Bear flung the door open to the astonishment of two female co-eds in short shorts and tight tank tops, nipples clearly present. Bear stared at the girl's chests for a moment before he found his voice.

"Oh hey. Sorry. What can we do you for? Is it cold in here, baby?" Bear yelled the last part back to Dakota in his best Austin Power's voice. The girls at first looked perturbed, but when Dakota came to the door…also shirtless and only wearing shorts, they got silly and giggly.

"Um, do either one of you have an extra iPhone charger. I totally can't find mine yet and my phone is almost dead," one of the girls, a pretty blonde, said.

"I might," Dakota said turning to look through his desk drawer. Bear walked over to his desk and brought back a cord.

"Here you go, ladies. Hope this helps. I'm Bear...and this is Dakota."

The girl looked skeptical at the cord and frustrated that it came from this towering giant in front of her. But his sweet smile and kindness won them over and soon they were chatting and being flirty with Bear and promised to return the cord the next day.

"Damn, nice titties," Bear said.

"They were just pretty in general...not just because their nips were all perky," Dakota said admonishing his roommate.

"Okay, okay. Stop trying to make me into Donald Trump just because I mentioned the nips. You know you saw them too," Bear said defensively.

Dakota patted the big player on the back. "Yeah, I noticed them for sure."

The guys went back to their respective desks, putting on headphones, and sending notes to the family back home. The light in the dorm room grew dim and soon, Dakota was yawning and wondering what time it was. He looked at his phone.

"Shit, it's almost 11:00. We better sleep, bro. Big day tomorrow. First practice and all that," the blond punter said gathering up his stuff and stowing it away in the desk drawer. He walked around to the other side of the beds to see Bear leaning over on his mattress, studying the thin privacy barrier in between the beds.

"What the hell is this supposed to be, bubba? I mean, what's the point? Like some tiny six inches of drywall is supposed to keep you from reaching over and giving me a handy in the middle of the night? Shit!"

Bear climbed up on his bed and studied the privacy wall in more detail. He gripped it and wiggled it slightly and the entire thing cracked off the screws holding it in place and banged to the floor, breaking off corners and shattering into several pieces.

"Oh fuck!" both boys shouted in unison. They stood staring at the broken barrier and then looked at one another and fell over laughing.

"Now you've done it. Now there's nothing to prevent you from raping my ass in the middle of the night," Dakota snapped.

"I know, and I could tell you were gonna put in one of those glory holes so you could suck me off easier."

"There goes the room deposit," Dakota said in fake indignation.

"Oh, we were never gonna get that back anyway, brother," Bear said. "But, Dude, I am sorry. You want to try and push these beds apart or put them on separate sides of the room or something?"

Dakota walked around the beds from one side to the other with Bear, looking at the setup and seeing if they could reconfigure it. They even tried to shove Bear's bed over to the wall, but it seemed ridiculously heavy and unwieldy. Finally they just stopped and looked at the room, hands on their hips.

"Man, I don't see how to rework this room," Bear said. "I guess maintenance can come put up another glory hole board."

"Yeah, make sure you call it that when you ask them to come," Dakota laughed. "You know, I like the set up here with having our study area separate and the beds in the middle. I mean, it's sort of stupid and makes it like we are practically sharing some big bed together, but honestly, it's no big deal to me. You don't snore do you?"

Bear gave Dakota a skeptical look. "Maybe," he said. "What about you, bro?"

"Hell if I know. But yeah, I probably do some."

"Fuck it, man. Let's worry about it later. That flimsy thing was bound to fall off sooner than later with you and me dry humping it all night long and everything."

Dakota patted Bear's large bicep. "Gotta tell you, brother. You scare me a little sometimes."

"Really? Well shit. I've never been scary before. That's cool."

They stood at the sink together and brushed their teeth. They went over a few more rules as they did.

"Okay, so if you have to piss in the middle of the night…do we flush or not flush?" Dakota asked with a mouth full of toothpaste.

"Hmm, I say don't flush. Then in the morning we send it on down."

"Agreed. "So when we need to drop a deuce…door locked?"

"Yeah sure. I mean, sorry about that earlier tonight."

"No, seriously, it didn't bother me at all. For a big ole guy, your shit doesn't really stink."

"Oh just wait, my man. It can be deadly sometimes. Check. Take a dump – lock it up."

Bear swished his mouth and spat in the sink, rinsing out the basin. "No toothpaste crud left in the sink."

"Agreed. No shit stains left in the toilet?"

"Affirmative. No pissing with the seat down?"

"Copy," Dakota agreed. "And no jizz left on the walls of the shower?"

"Hell to the No!" Bear barked with a laugh. "Now let's get to the important shit."

"Like what?"

"When do I get a turn with your Fleshlight?"

Dakota's face flushed red. "Eat me."

"Why sir, whatever do you mean," Bear said fluttering his hand in front of his face like a fan, using his best southern belle accent.

"I'm glad you mentioned that thing. I better wash it out," Dakota said retrieving the sex toy and bringing it over to the sink.

"Now don't be too hasty. Sloppy seconds sounds pretty sexy, bro."

"You have a diseased mind," Dakota said unscrewing the toy to wash it out.

"Says the boy fucking a pocket pussy."

"Hey, this isn't the pussy attachment," Dakota said with a fake sense of anger, "It's the sexy mouth attachment." Bear picked up the soft vinyl lips and ran his large finger across the mouth and inside, making Dakota cringe a bit, his face blushing again. Bear pulled his cock from his underwear and slid the mouth over his large mushroom head halfway down his thick shaft. He stood in front of the mirror and shook his hips back and forth, wearing the mouth attachment like a necklace on his dick.

"Oh my God," Dakota said shielding his eyes.

"You know, I bet that thing really is fun to use. You are gonna share, right?"

"I don't know man...it's like sharing a butt plug with someone."

"You've got a butt plug too?" Bear asked in wonder.

"Oh for God's sake," Dakota said laughing.

"You know..." Bear began, taking the lips off his cock and studying them closely. "This mouth looks like someone I know. I think these lips look like Tom Brady's mouth."

"You are insane," Dakota said pulling the toy from Bear's hand to rinse it off. He looked at the lips and a slight realization crossed his face. Bear hooted.

"See? What did I tell you? Those lips wrap around Gronk and Julian Edelman's cocks when they are on the road roommates.

"I rather doubt that," Dakota said and yet he couldn't push the image of perfect Brady swallowing his two receiver's loads before a big game now.

"You a Pats fan?" Dakota said to change the subject.

"Fuck no. I mean, I appreciate how great they are and all that, but I'm Seahawks all the way. What about you?"

"Yeah, Hawks are great. Kind of like the Titans now, what with Marcus Mariota being the QB and all."

"Well, he's great. That team is shit, though. I kind of like the Pack. Hate Giants, Skins, Rams, and Cards for sure," Bear said with a fury, punching his fist into this other hand.

"Such rage, brother," Dakota said drying off the Fleshlight and tossing it back to Bear. "There you go, ready for your big nut. If that giant cock of yours will even fit."

Bear studied the toy again. "Not sure I'll get off more feeding Brady my dick or...he picked up the asshole attachment...or sliding it into J.J.'s bunghole here."

"Oh, so that looks like J.J. Watt's asshole to you?"

"Well, he's a real smooth guy. Not hairy like me or even like you. And this pucker..." he held the vinyl anus up beside his face, pursing his lips like a cat's butt, "looks like a guy who doesn't have to shave his asshole."

"I have no response to any of that."

"See, I might say this pretty pucker could be your boy Mariota's...but let's face it, he's got to have a nice furry bunghole, don't you think?

"Actually, I have never thought about that at all." Dakota said with an air of superiority that seemed lost on Bear. It also was a total lie.

Dakota had spent more than one long jack-off session wondering exactly what Marcus would look like in and out of his jock.

"Okay, man. You don't have to make me feel like a total homo perv over here," Bear said, actually a bit hurt, it seemed to Dakota.

"I'm just breaking your balls, roomie. It's fine if you want it to be J.J.'s butthole...or whomever you want to bang. I guess I figured they wanted you to think this is a girl's asshole, though."

"You know, it's funny, but I don't usually think about girl's assholes. Seems unkind or something to me, you know, to fuck a girl up her shitter."

"I think plenty of guys feel way differently than you on that. Around my school, guys fucked girls in the ass all the time because you couldn't get them pregnant that way."

"This is true, but butt sex has just always seemed like a thing two gays do instead a girl and boy. Okay, shit...I am beat, bro. Let's go to sleep."

"I'm with you," Dakota said stepping into the bathroom. He stood in front of the toilet and pissed loudly into the bowl. He looked over and saw Bear standing there holding his dick.

"Want to sword fight?"

Dakota shook his head but jumped around and watched Bear's urine stream blast into the toilet, the two of them crossing streams back and forth as they pissed.

"Me and my big bro used to do this all the time back home. Well, when we were smaller and all," Bear said. The guys finished and Bear flushed, patting Dakota on his ass as he walked past. "Thanks for being cool with me and everything today, man. I know, I'm a country bumpkin and all that. Like just then, with peeing at the same time, I bet plenty of guys would have just punched me in the throat or told me I was a big raging queer or something. You just don't get bent out of shape that much."

Dakota smiled. "Hey, everyone's weird in one way or the other. I've got plenty of crazy shit I deal with and I am sure you will learn about it soon enough. I don't care if you haul out your dong and piss with me...just, don't do it in the locker room or when other guys are around, please."

"It'll be our secret," Bear said moving in to give Dakota a kiss on the cheek.

The punter yelped and dodged his lips and went over to his side of the room to get into bed. The beds were elevated on top of the dresser drawers and their desks. But beside the desk was a step that helped you in and out of the bed without feeling like you were having to do the high jump just to get in. Dakota shook his head as he saw Bear simply lay down, he was so tall he didn't need the step-up. Dakota walked around the beds again and flipped off the light and then bounded into the bed, colliding with Bear in the middle of where the beds adjoined.

"Oof, bro. You kneed me right in the nuggets," Bear said groaning, writhing around holding his balls."

"Sorry, Bear. We've got to deal with this thing. I mean, the way it is right now, there's a four-inch gap that we are both going to roll into in the middle of the night."

"Maybe we should try and push them closer instead of apart, that way, there won't be a hole to fall into."

"Shit. Let's try it," Dakota said climbing out of the bed. The guys huffed and strained and pushed and finally got the beds right against each other. "Okay, that's probably better. Damn, if people come in our room they are gonna go ape shit...us all cozy together in one big bed."

"Yeah, I know. But we could always just hop into the other guy's bed and fuck and then get back in our own. I mean, that probably happens in other dorm rooms here sometimes, don't you think?"

Dakota smiled and fist bumped his roomie. "Spoken like a true renaissance man. Not bad for a country bumpkin." The guys climbed back into bed after Dakota turned off the light. The glow from their respective phones lit up the room. They lay on their backs, scrolling through messages on their phones. Their faces were tinted blue in the light of the phones. Suddenly, Bear sat up.

"Oh shit, sorry forgot something." He hopped down, rummaged around in a Rubbermaid tote and brought back a clip-on fan that he attached to his headboard and turned on, blowing down on his pillow. Bear looked back at Dakota ready to make an apology for the fan when he saw Dakota bring up a similar one and clip to his bed. "Oh man, now I know this is marriage made in heaven. 'Cause there ain't no way I can sleep without the fan noise and wind."

Dakota lay back with his hands under his head. "Yeah, I was sweating that. Glad you are a normal guy like me." Dakota's smooth chest and belly glowed in the light of the phones, his sheet pushed down to his ankles. "Still kind of hot in here tonight." Bear mirrored the action, kicking his sheet and blanket down to the foot of his bed. Dakota could feel the radiant heat from the big long snapper's body against his own skin as they lay beside each other, no more than two or three inches apart.

"You gonna be okay us sleeping close like this, bro," Bear said into the darkened room. They could hear random doors close and occasional loud voices in the hallway.

"Yeah. I'm so tired, I don't even think I will notice."

"For what it's worth, man. I'm kind of digging this bed set up."

"Why's that?" Dakota asked turning on his side. He pulled his head back when he came eye to eye with the big freshman across from him. Both the guys laughed.

"Ah, you'll just think I'm a bigger pussy country boy than you do already," Bear said looking at Dakota with sincerity.

"No I won't. What do you mean?"

"Okay, look. I've shared a bedroom my whole life with my big bro. He's still not married and so he's still there. And probably until he got into high school, we slept in the same bed. We just got used to it and our house isn't that big and it's just how it was. So, I guess I was a little worried on how it was gonna feel to be on my own and all that. It's like a million times better than I thought it would be with you being so cool and easy. So, there. I know I'm a big puss and homo, but I'm glad you are right there beside me. It feels, I don't know, right."

Dakota reached out and ruffled Bear's thick black hair. "I've slept by myself forever. I always wanted a brother and it never happened. So for what it's worth, I am just as happy to have a big goob like you right here beside me too. Because I was very worried about being homesick and kind of on edge and everything. From the minute you walked in on me and my little friend...I got the idea we are gonna be fine together."

Bear reached over and gave Dakota a Dutch Rub.

"You probably want to knock off calling yourself or me a homo though. Now that we are in college, there are going to be plenty of people that get offended with that, even though I know you don't mean it in a hateful way."

"You're right, bro. See, I need a city guy like you to be my filter. So, you kinda think we can be bros, huh bro?"

"Yeah,"

"Does that mean I get to have a turn with your pocket pussy soon?"

Dakota roared. "You want it right now, man?"

"Nah, I might be too tired to even stroke it tonight, man. So...that does bring up a fairly obvious question though."

Dakota nodded his head. "No privacy, so how you gonna beat off and all that?"

"Well, clearly you have shown the shower is a great option since you painted the walls with your nut butter."

"I'm sorry about that. But, no doubt, we both spank it at other times than just in the shower. Do we come up with a signal on the door or just work it out when the other guy is in class or what?"

"Those are fine, I mean, we aren't gonna be in every class together. And since we have already navigated what happens when you get walked in on...I doubt we would fall apart if that happens again. I will admit, I pretty much rub one off every night to fall asleep. So that might be the major adjustment."

"Yeah, for me too," Dakota said turning over on his side. Now his right arm and shoulder were actually touching Bear's.

"Well, we don't have to crack this nut before bed tonight, but bubba, if you wake up here in an hour and my bunk is rockin'... don't go a-knockin'. Unless you are gonna give me a reach-around."

"Preach, brother," Dakota said holding up his fist again, this time after they bumped, they wiggled their fingers against each other's.

The guys lay quietly for a few minutes, the hum from the dual fans filling the room. The other noises from other rooms calmed down. Dakota looked over and Bear was on his back, his arms tucked behind his head. His great black tufts of armpit hair were fluffed out like a stuffed animal. Dakota could still feel the heat from Bear's body against his own and smell the soap and slight musky odor from his pits. It caused his dick to swell and he pushed it back down.

"Hey Koda? Is it okay for me to call you, Koda?"

Dakota snickered. "Um, okay B. Guess we can go with the nicknames."

"Cool. So, I gotta ask...those guys back at the park. You ever, you know, try anything like that before?"

Dakota laughed. "Nope, not even close. What about you, big guy?"

"Nothing like that. I mean, you know, a couple of touchy-feely things with my bro and a friend back in school. Playing doctor when you're a kid and stuff, but fuck, I never did anything like those dudes. That older guy, he was wearing a wedding ring too."

"And I doubt he was married to another guy. I guess some guys just need some D on the side or something."

"I sometimes wondered about my old man and this fishing and hunting bud of his."

Dakota looked over. "You really think your dad goes all Brokeback with his friend?"

Bear lay quiet for a minute and then turned on his side. "I kind of saw them fooling around one time. My bro and I were in our own tent out camping. Dad and Gene were in their tent. I got up to take a piss in the night and heard funny sounds from their tent. I sneaked over and peeked inside and they were head to toe, you know, I think doing the ole six-nine."

"Shut the fuck up."

"Yeah, I mean, there was my dad's balls and his big cock all the way in Gene's mouth and him grunting and dumping his nads in the guys mouth. I freaked out and ran back to the tent."

"Holy shit. What did you do? Did you tell your brother?"

"Fucking-A. I told him and he was real weird about it like maybe he already knew. He looked down and saw my dick was all hard and he thumped it and said, 'Well don't be rubbing one off and shooting your jizz all over the tent.' And I just lay there stunned, finally asking him 'You think they do that a lot?' and my bro just turns over with this funny grin and says 'He sure goes hunting and camping a lot now, don't he?' I didn't know what to make of that but I just figured he must already have known."

"Holy shit. That would be so crazy. Since my dad and mom split up, he sometimes hangs out with this guy Paul a lot. I have wondered about that too, but I really doubt it. So what did you do after seeing that and all?"

"Just jacked off."

Dakota laughed. "Right there beside your bro?"

"Hell yeah. It sure as fuck wasn't the first time. He was spanking his by that time too."

"Jesus. You should have just jerked each other."

"Amen to that," Bear said.

Five minutes later, Bear was softly snoring on his side, his large back close to Dakota's, their backsides almost touching. He let his hand drift over and casually brush against the long snapper's soft boxer briefs that hugged his large ass, letting his fingers gently touch the thick black hairs that covered his thighs. Just feeling him there made Dakota feel happy and safe, and noticing his stiff cock, clearly aroused. Dakota drifted off to sleep with his hand resting on Bear's thigh.

Bear's eyes opened slightly and he smiled, scooting his butt over closer to Dakota's, feeling the warmth of his roomie's hand on his leg as he fell back asleep.

6. First Practice

The roommates sat beside one another in the large lecture hall with the rest of the team. Coach Johnson was going through a long list of rules, schedules, and expectations before the head coach took over. Bear sat on the aisle with Dakota beside him. To the other side of Dakota was Connor Tuafila, the place kicker with Dillon Cox the kickoff guy. Further down the row, LaDarius Jenkins, Elmo Fonda, and DeQuan Bishop slunk low in their seats, the trio of punt and kickoff return backs that made up the special teams unit. LaDarius and DeQuan were juniors, having distinguished themselves as some of the best punt returners in the Division II system. They both sported large diamond earrings in both ears, that shown bright against the smooth dark brown skin of their ears. Elmo Fonda was a freshman like Dakota and Bear. He was small, five foot five, but solid muscle and strong as an ox. His fiery red hair stood out amongst all the brown and black afros and shaved heads along with the smattering of blond and sandy brown hair on the white guys. Conner was a sophomore, but had already made the short-list for all-American kickers last year with a near perfect PAT and field goal percentage. His longest field goal had been a shattering 53 yards and won the Wolf Pack the game against Pacific University last year. Conner was part Samoan, part Hawaiian, and at 6-4, one of the biggest kickers in all college football. He had a winning smile and gentle spirit, which was juxtaposed with his stylistic short cropped hair with the pattern trimmed into the sides as well as long tattoo sleeves on each arm and designs across his chest.

Dakota looked over at Bear who was doodling in his notebook. Beside several notes he had made concerning tickets for family, warnings about inappropriate social media posts, and the dangers of drinking and dating and sexual violence, he had drawn a comic penis with fluffy fur around it and the words: Coach Harry Johnson in the margin.

"You better not let anyone see that," Dakota whispered from the side of his mouth.

"I won't, but it's his name so what's the big deal. Damn, I wish they would shut up and let us go practice. My ass is tired of sitting."

"So just remember, fellas...you do not want to be on the news because of a racist, sexist, or defamatory tweet or Facebook post. Shit on the internets lives forever. It won't matter if you were just teasing or joking. It won't matter if you just liked some rude or provocative post, the media and fans will crucify you for it. So welcome to the real world, men. If you snap a quick photo of your Johnson for your sweet thing back home or here on campus, it's only a matter of time before it ends up on Deadspin or ESPN or worse. Just ask yourself every time you get ready to post something...am I prepared to get interviewed on television and defend what I just posted? If you don't want to do that, then for fuck's sake, don't post it. Be professional, respectful, and kind. It goes without saying, but we have zero tolerance for any hazing or bullying of any kind. And if you get involved in any kind of domestic abuse or sexual drama with your 'bae, you will get released from this team. Got it?"

There was a murmur of agreement. Coach Johnson gathered up his things to make way for the head coach. Coach Taylor was a large, solid man with a Jeff Fisher goatee and a calm exterior. He went over the week's schedule and daily routine expectations before reiterating half of what Coach Johnson had already said. Dakota and Bear fidgeted back and forth in their seats. Dakota's phone buzzed and he peeked at the screen. It was another fucking Grindr text:

Hey you must be in this never-ending team meeting with me. Shit, do we dare try and figure out who each other is? BTW, great armpit pic.

Bear literally pulled Dakota's phone out of his hand and stared at the screen with wide eyes before Dakota snatched it back.

"Dick!" Dakota hissed under his breath.

"Who is sexting you, bro? Does that mean it's someone on the team? Does he know it's you?"

"I don't know. Be quiet, man," Dakota said pocketing his phone. He casually looked around the large room wondering who just texting him, feeling his balls contract and his dick swell.

"It's pretty cool to think there's some guy out there all flirty and all with you."

"You better knock it off or I am gonna brain you," Dakota said out of the side of his mouth.

The coach finally finished up and dismissed the team to head off to their various functional breakouts. Not surprisingly, special teams was sent to a tiny cluttered office off the weight room. Dakota and Bear filed into the small room with the kicker and punt and kickoff guys. A beefy young coach entered closing the door.

"Hey men. I'm Coach Kelly. Glad you are all with us. We've got a great bunch of talent in here, even if it is really young. Got two of the best return guys in the state here. Big shout out to LaDarius, DeQuan, and Elmo. Got the state champion punter there. How's it going, Dakota. There's a highly recruited long snapper, Bear McLeod. Of course, our returning place kicker, Connor Tuafila. And lucky for us, we picked up a great kick off man, Dillon Cox so our field goal man can specialize a bit more. Obviously, a number of offense and defense guys will also be joining us on kick offs and punts and field goal, but they have their own meetings right now. You guys are the heart and soul of special teams. I know, it's hard to feel the love sometimes when you are the long snapper. But I tell you, Bear...without you being at the top of your game and snapping that ball just right for Dakota or Connor, we are fucked. So regardless of whether or not you get all the sexy accolades of the QB, running backs, or receivers, just know you are super important. And more than that, Coach Johnson and Kelly will get butt hurt like you have never seen and come after you with guns blazing if you fuck up things for the team. So on that cheery note, let's talk some play basics."

The coach ran some video and talked over good and bad special teams plays and even outlined several schemes he was going to implement for the year. The discussion when on for almost an hour before it was time to break for lunch.

"Okay men. Go get some lunch. Then back to the field house. Grab your jocks, socks, and cocks and meet on the field, north end zone and we will start practice.   "

Dakota and Bear moved out of the small room and headed off to the cafeteria with the other special team players. They must have beaten the others out of their meetings and breezed through the chow line in only a few minutes. The guys sat with the other special teams players and got better acquainted. Bear sat and began to joke and chat with Dillon. The small back looked like a grade school boy sitting next to the monstrous Bear, but the stocky red head was confident and funny and seemed to enjoy the chance to get to know the big long snapper whose plate was heaped with protein and salad. Dakota sat next to Bear with Connor on the other side. Dakota's long legs rubbed against Bear's huge leg on the one side and touched Connor's solid, muscled tan leg on the other. Dakota searched his mind for something to chat with Conner about.

"Um, Connor. What island are you from?" He hoped that was a good thing to ask someone. He felt like a moron with certain small talk etiquette.

"Big Island," Connor said with a mouthful of fajita chicken wrap."

"Oh cool. My dad and I went there after my graduation for a vacation. What part?"

"Puako."

"Really? That's like right where we stayed. Our condo was down in the Waikola Resort area."

"Sweet. Really nice there. You like snorkeling?"

"I love it. Finally figured out the stand-up paddleboarding too. Took me a whole day. I was a real spaz with that at first."

"Lots of Haoles can't figure that shit out."

"Haole?"

"White people," Connor answered stuffing more food in his mouth. Dakota chuckled but felt weird and figured this must be the way lots of non-white people felt all the time.

"We went on a night snorkel trip, swam with the mantas."

"That's cool. I have never done that. So, you and Big Bear...you guys been friends for a while?"

"What? Oh, no. Just met yesterday."

"He's a big guy."

"Yeah, he is," Dakota said with a grin. "Real big"

Connor looked at Dakota and slowly nodded. "How big," he asked in a low voice.

Dakota picked up his fajita wrap and held it down in his lap, gripping the huge 10 inch log tortilla with both hands. Connor smiled and gave a hang-loose sign with his thumb and little finger outstretched.

"I figured. That's cool, brah. Elmo might be a little guy, but he packing, you feel me."

Dakota looked over at the small redhead yakking away with Bear and smiled. "Yeah, big things come in small packages, huh?"

"Yeah, sure do. Not that I been peeking, you know."

"Exactly," Dakota said enjoying the flirty banter and the knowledge that he wasn't the only guy on the team that took notice of an impressive penis.

"I'm gonna go get some hot sauce. You want anything?"

"I'm good, but thanks, man," Dakota said. He waited until the kicker left the table and pulled out his phone again. He looked at the last Grindr text and then clicked open the photo attached. It was a torso shot of a well-defined six-pack, smooth belly with a small tail of fur leading from the navel down toward unseen pubes. The skin was fairly light and even slightly freckled. He looked closely at the belly and even slid the photo to enlarge it and as it did so, a thought entered his mind. He quickly texted back:

>"You enjoying that big burrito. Why you drinking a Red Bull?"

Dakota pressed send and quickly slid his phone into his pocket. He resumed eating, pretending to be nonchalant and focused on lunch. But he scanned right out of the corner of his eye and watched the player just down the table from him react to a text coming in. The player casually glanced at his phone, almost dropping his wrap as he did. He sat the food down and spun his neck around back and forth scanning the cafeteria for something. His red hair blew around his head as he turned from side to side.

"Who you looking for, bro," Bear said.

Elmo Fonda sat across from Bear. He covered his phone screen and studied the text and quickly sent back another message. Dakota's asshole contracted as his phone buzzed in his pocket. *Bingo*, he thought. He didn't dare reach for his phone, but smiled at the bit of spy work that had solved the small mystery. *Guess he wasn't the only guy who enjoyed taking a peek at some peen once in a while*, he thought.

Connor was coming back to the table with his hot sauce. Dakota noticed the boy's large package was loosely swinging back and forth in the thin shorts he wore. Dakota pressed his legs together to try and will his cock to behave and not react to the endless stimuli around his teammates. Bear's big arm slid around his shoulders.

"You ready to kick the shit out of some balls, bro?" he said, his breath spicy and oniony from the lunch.

"Yeah, if I can get a decent snap from a slacker like you," he said, nudging Bear in the ribs. Bear's hand patted his thigh dangerously close to his balls.

"No worries, buddy. I got you. You got my six?"

Dakota laughed. "Yep – all I do is stare at your six when you're all bent over ready to hike that ball." Bear roared.

"What are you laughing about?" Dillon asked from the other side of Bear.

"Oh, just my punter roomie here, telling me how much he enjoys staring at my big ole ass and sack when he's ready to kick the ball."

"Well, it's sure a big enough target to stare at, huh?" Dillion said holding up a fist to bump against Dakota.

"Word!" Dakota said. He watched Elmo across the table take out his phone and quickly text another message, feeling his ass buzz again from his phone in his pocket. Dakota grinned and finished up his food. He stood to leave, leaning over to Bear.

"I'm gonna run back to the room right before heading over to practice."

"Gonna go drop off the Browns at the Super Bowl?" Bear said with a full mouth.

"Can't keep anything from you, bro. See you." He tapped Connor on the shoulder and waved goodbye and put his tray away. He sprinted out of the cafeteria and walked briskly back to the dorm, looking at his phone as he walked.

> Hey man – where are you. It's cool, not like I'm gonna tell or anything.
> How did you know it was me?

Dakota texted back:

> Lucky guess – saw that hot red fur on your belly

A moment later:

> Look who's so smart, Encyclopedia Brown. You gonna give me a hint?

Dakota texted back:

> Soon. BTW, I love red hair. Bet your dick looks tasty.

A moment later:

> I'd be glad to show you in person, dude.

Dakota replied:

> Sweet. If you mean it, and want to meet, I would do that. But FYI – I am totally DL on this. Not interested in being Michael Sam

A moment later:

> Copy – same here. Great, now my dick is gonna be all fat and sassy during practice. Thanks! LOL

Dakota replied

> Can't wait to see that baby in the locker room. ☺

A moment later – a big full color photo of a fat cock surrounded by a thick nest of trimmed red pubes filled the screen of his phone. Dakota studied the pic, sliding his hand down to stroke his dick as he did. He opened his photos and selected one and sent it back. It was a closeup of his own penis, heavy and full, but not rock hard, laying on top of his big balls.

A moment later:

➢ Fucking hot man. You are really big.

Dakota unlocked his room and went to the bathroom, sliding his shorts down and sitting on the john. He opened his Tumblr app and scrolled through new posts from Daddy Issues and Jocks, Socks, and Cocks. The photos of the young guys down between older men's legs sucking big dicks or bent over for Dad's to plow them caused his dick to grow hard as he took a dump. There were pics of guys fucking girls or eating pussy, he looked at them and then moved on to the next set: these of jock-strapped guys eating each other's ass. The door to the dorm opened and Bear came in, followed by Dillon Cox. Dakota reached for the bathroom door to push it closed, but couldn't reach it from the toilet.

"Oh damn. Sorry to walk in on you pinching a loaf, bro. I was grabbing my lucky t-shirt," Bear said waving like an idiot. Connor stood in the doorway grinning.

"You got the right idea, man. I ought to go take a shit before we get going with practice."

"Yeah, that's what I'm trying to do here."

Dillon stepped into the bathroom and pointed at Dakota's phone screen. The photo of a big breasted girl sucking a big black cock was shining brightly. The player pulled the phone from Dakota's hand.

"Jesus, look at her tits and fuck, that guy is huge. I bet ole DeQuan has a big dick like that." He scrolled through some more photos, his eyes bulging as he got to another set of guys sucking dad or getting fucked in the ass by a jock-strapped top.

"Woah, man. Some of these pics are really gay. Shit, look at them chow down on each other. Shit, dude. You are all equal-opportunity porn guy, huh? Fuck, that's some crazy shit."

Dakota's face was scarlet. He pulled the phone back. "Tumblr gives you all kinds of crazy pics sometime. Uh, do you mind? Maybe a little privacy while I wipe my ass?"

"Oh sorry, man. I know what you mean. Elmo walks in on me all the time and we just met. He caught me jacking off yesterday."

Bear bellowed from the other room. "Oh snap...I walked in on Koda too."

Dakota winced. "Thanks roomie!" Dillon laughed and closed the door to the bathroom. Dakota wiped his butt and flushed. He had already had more guys standing around watching him take a shit than he had in his whole life and it was barely day two. Part of him hated it and part of him loved that he was close enough and comfortable enough with teammates that even something as personal as taking a crap was shared. Dakota came out to find Dillon standing in front of Bear, his shorts and underwear down, showing the big player a fresh tattoo that was still red and inflamed. It was a small wolf head tatt that lay just to the right of his dick, just outside the tidy brown nest of pubes.

"Check out Dilly's new ink, bro," Bear said. Bear traced the outline of the wolf head with his finger. Dillon's penis lay two inches away, full and heavy, on top of big golf ball sized nuts in a tight sack. "Dude, does it still hurt?"

Dillon stood with his hands on his hips, submitting to Bear's touches and Dakota's inspection with no ill ease. "It's a little tender. You guys have any tatts?"

"I don't," Bear said. "You don't either, do you Koda?"

"Actually, I do," the blond punter said pulling off his t-shirt and flexing his bicep showing off the small Celtic knot band that circled his muscle. "Oh, and this one too," he said, sliding down his shorts to reveal a small Hawaiian fishhook in almost the exact same place to the right of his dick and pubes as Dillon. The smaller kicker reached out and ran his finger over the tatt before Bear did the same, grinning at Dakota and pretending to grab his cock in the process. Dakota pulled away.

"How did I not see this yesterday?" Bear said.

"Guess you were too busy staring at my ass instead."

"It is a great ass," Bear said with fake awe. Dillon laughed.

"Man, you guys are crazy. We better split."

The afternoon was brutal. It was hot and non-stop. Even the special teams guys were run ragged. They did stretches, regular warm-up exercise, wind sprints and even ran the bleaches for a short time. The team was dripping with sweat with chests heaving at the end of that. The groups broke and began to run drills. The kickers and snappers moved to the sidelines or far end zones and began to work on snaps. Dakota stood behind Bear and called for the snap. The ball sailed into his hands perfectly, burning his fingers, as he popped off a fifty yard punt. They ran through twenty minutes of punting practice, Dakota staring intently at the wide ass bent over in front of him, Bear's huge balls hanging low in the shorts. For some reason, he felt happy just knowing this big oaf in front of him all bent over was his roommate and new friend. Connor sat on the ground stretching, watching the two work. Dakota saw that Connor was staring at Bear's backside as intently as he was. From the looks of the bulge in his shorts, the kicker was as impressed by the big kid's balls as he was.

The coach called for them to change up, and Connor moved into place, with Dakota now taking the snap and setting the ball for place kicks. Bear centered the ball cleanly and Dakota caught the snap, placed the ball, spinning the laces around, and feeling Connor move up to kick the field goal. It was clean from 35 yards.

"Nice one, Connor," Coach Kelly said. Let's move it back and try 40 now."

The guys continued the practice, moving back ever so many kicks until Connor was consistently hitting 50 yard field goals.

"That's great work guys. It will be interesting to see how you do when we get the defense in your face. Okay, Bear, I want you and Dakota to work on snaps with him under center. He will be functioning as back up QB if we ever got to that place as well as passing on gadget plays, fake punts, you name it. Get that snap count and hand-off clean."

The guys moved over to the edge of the end zone, Connor staying back to practice more kicks with the stand. Bear moved into position, crouching low with his legs wide spread, looking back to see Dakota.

"Not from the shotgun, man." Bear barked. "Get your hands under my legs."

Dakota moved up behind Bear's large rear and leaned in, his hands hovering under his wide-spread legs. Dakota called for the ball. It hit his hands and bounced out."

"Hey! Clean that shit up over there. No drops, Dakota!" Coach Kelly shouted.

Bear stood and turned around, a frown on his face.

"Dude. Get your hands down between my legs. You gotta rest your hands on my sack, man. I have to feel you there to know when to snap. You've done that before, right?"

"Um, we mostly did shotgun stuff. Not really used to being under center."

"Well, you better get used to it, fucker!" The big man bent over again, Dakota moved up and slid his hands under Bear's ass, resting his right hand on his balls just barely. He called for the snap and pulled away to do a three step drop. He managed to keep the ball but it looked clumsy.

"Keep working it. That better look perfect by tomorrow, boys," Coach Kelly said clearly perturbed.

By the end of practice, the players were exhausted and they weren't even in pads or facing a defense. Dakota and Bear stood near one another in the shower after practice, not talking, just trying to cool down and clean up. The steamy shower room was massive, with twenty stainless shower columns blasting out warm water, four large shower heads to the pole. Bear and Dakota shared a shower with a tall, 6-7 tight end named Alex and a muscled defensive end named Leon who was 6-4. They were muscled and hard bodied, some of the upper classmen. Alex sported a wedding ring on his left hand. The players chatted as they washed up, casually soaping their pits and bellies and spending plenty of time with their cock and balls. Both men were well hung, Alex cut with low hanging balls, Leon uncut with a generous foreskin that he brazenly retracted and washed underneath. Bear and Dakota attempted to keep their eyes on their own business, but stole glances whenever they could.

"How you rookies doing?" Leon bellowed over the loud chatting and laughter from the shower room.

Bear shouted back. "All good. Pretty tired."

"Shit. That ain't nothing.' Damn, rook! How big are you anyway?"

"Uh, I don't know. About nine inches or so I think."

The upper classmen roared. "Fool, I was asking how tall you were not about yo' cock. Damn!" Both of the older players grabbed their dicks and began to wiggle them at Bear. Alex spoke with a country accent.

"Lookie here. I got a huge pecker," he said with a thick twang. Bear laughed along with the older teammates but Dakota saw the bright red flush down his neck. He might have just met Bear, but it didn't take a psychologist to know he was very embarrassed. The older players left the shower room, laughing and shaking their heads. Dakota moved closer until his arm was touching Bear's as the player absent-mindedly soaped his balls. Dakota was again in awe of the young man's impressive junk.

"Hey, don't mind them. They're just jealous of your horse cock, bro," Dakota whispered.

"Just leave me alone, Dakota," Bear said turning to leave the shower. Dakota rolled his eyes and poured shampoo in his hair and lathered it up. He looked across the shower and spied a bright red head. The guy was solid and perfectly proportioned. His muscles were ripped and rolled on his biceps. His belly was flat and his six-pack defined. He slowly slid his hand back and forth on his cock. Dakota looked up and saw Elmo staring straight at him. Dakota gave him a weak smile and turned off his shower and grabbed a towel to wrap around his waist. He looked back to see the small running back still softly stroking his hardening cock, a piercing stare on his face.

Dakota dressed and headed back to the dorm. Finding it empty, he changed into a new shirt and shorts and flip flops and headed to the cafeteria. He scanned the large room for any sign of Bear but didn't see him. He grabbed his shepherd's pie and took a seat at an empty table. He pulled out his phone and found Bear's number that he had only added last night.

> Where are you?

His phone remained silent. A large guy moved in front of him at the table. Dakota looked up to see Blake Preston, the team's senior QB standing in front of him with his tray.

"Mind if I join you, Dakota?"

Dakota swallowed and gestured to the seat. "Sure. Make yourself at home."

"Thanks. I don't normally eat in the cafeteria anymore but during football training, coach tells me to hang out and schmooze. So I'm gonna schmooze with you. Sounds dirty, huh?"

Dakota laughed. "You can probably schmooze with anyone you want, you're the team captain. Everyone knows who you are."

"Which is both cool and a total pain in the ass. Man, you can't scratch your balls without someone watching you or making a comment. So, where's you big roommate. The Bear?"

"Not sure. I just texted him," Dakota said forking up a mouthful of food. It tasted pretty good.

"He's a huge guy. Man, you probably run into each other in that tiny dorm room. I remember when I was freshman. My roomie and I got pretty sick of one another. He was a funny guy. He was a back-up QB and never been away from home. The first weekend here, I woke up and he was curled up in my bed snuggling with me."

Dakota snorted and took a drink. "That's crazy."

"Ah, he was just homesick, I think. But when I think back now, I think he might have actually had a little crush on me or something."

"Wow. Did you kick him out of the bed?"

"Nah, I just got up and got in his bed. Which was fine but smelled like cum cause I swear he jerked off on his sheets."

"Eww," Dakota said. "Get a cum rag, dude."

"Exactly. Hey looked good out there today, some long booming punts. But you and Bear gotta get better with snaps when you are under center. It's crucial you guys are ready for that when we need it. You probably haven't had your hands on a guy's nutsack much before. Always shotgun I bet."

"Yeah. That obvious, huh?"

"It takes some getting used to. When I was a freshman, my center was an upperclassman. He could tell I was shy and squeamish about resting my hand on his beanbag, so one day he made me come over to his apartment and he literally stripped down to his jock and made me hold my hand on his nuts for almost an hour. He taught me how to direct him and signal with the back of my hand or my fingers on his sack. It was super uncomfortable, but by the time I left, I was so used to holding his balls, I didn't even think about it. I think I held his balls way more than my own. Now with Nate, I grip his junk all the time. Sometimes, I have to yell at him cause my hand ends up smelling like ass and I cuss at him and tell him to get his hole cleaned up."

Dakota snorted and wiped his mouth. "How lovely."

"Well, we all smell pretty bad, but sweat and nut stank is different than a dirty asshole."

They talked for a few more minutes before Blake stood and said bye and moved over to another table. He was quite the politician, Dakota thought. He was handsome, talented, moved with ease and grace on the football field as well as in the lunchroom. Staring as he walked away, Dakota smiled at his round ass stuffed in way-too tight shorts, which gripped his cheeks and formed a smooth bulge around his cock. Damn. Dakota looked up and across the lunchroom a few tables over, Elmo Fonda stared at him again. His bright hair was wild and messy and he wore a dark blue tank top that showed off his impressive muscles and thick tufts of red armpit hair. Dakota raised his hand up in a quick hello before taking his tray to the turn-in window. As he left the lunch room, he could feel Elmo's eyes following him out the whole way. *Dang,* Dakota thought, *wonder if he's figured out who was texting him?*

Dakota spied the large, slow walking form of Bear across the quad as he moved toward the dorm. He jogged over and laid a hand on the tall player's broad shoulders. "Hey man. Missed you at dinner. You okay, B?"

Bear looked at him. His eyes were red-rimmed and he looked clearly upset. "Yeah. Fine."

"Hey hold it," Dakota said, holding out an arm to stop his roommate from walking. "You are way not fine. What's up, bro?"

"Nothing. Just a bad day." Bear walked toward the dorm room again. Dakota started to try and engage him again, but instead just followed in his shadow and into the room. The big man kicked off his flip flops and climbed into bed. Dakota plugged in his phone to the charger, noticing yet another text on his phone.

> - *Have fun chatting with QB1?*
> - *Yeah, he's cool.*
> - *He's got a nice ass*
> - *Yes he does*
> - *So do you – I enjoyed seeing you in all your glory in the shower. Damn*
> - *You're not so bad yourself*
> - *So you know who this is?*
> - *I think so, yeah. Guess you know me now too.*
> - *Yep – the fishhook tatt gave it away.*
> - *Oh shit. Well, we cool?*

> ➤ *Yep. Will you meet me tomorrow? Just have a chat?*
> ➤ *Sure. Have a good night.*
> ➤ *Hope you suck that big Bear cock tonight* ☺
> ➤ *Right*

Dakota turned around to see Bear laying on his back, his shorts sliding down his big thighs making them look almost like briefs. He casually stroked his balls, his legs spread wide apart, one hand behind his head. Dakota climbed into his bed and lay back on the pillow, his head close to Bear's.

"Want to talk about it?"

"Ah, not really."

"Okay. Well, if I can help somehow…"

What? You want to suck me off or something?"

"Huh? Hey why are you being a douchebag?"

Bear looked into Dakota's bright green eyes with a weary, sad expression. "Pay no attention to me, man. I'm fucked up."

"Why? What fucked you up, brother? Was it those asshole upperclassmen busting your balls in the shower?"

He nodded. "I'm such an idiot…9 inches! I mean, why did I think that?"

Dakota stifled a big laugh and simply smiled. "It was an honest mistake. That's what I thought they were getting at too. I mean, lots of guys notice your anaconda, man."

"There's guys on the team who have bigger cocks than I do."

"Maybe, but you've got the whole package man…big dick, big balls, hairy belly, huge monster muscles… Guys are going to notice you. Better than getting noticed for having a micropenis."

"Like that real pale O-Lineman. Jack or whatever. His dick was like two inches long and uncut. You couldn't even see it."

"Yeah, there you go. You look a million times better than that. Those guys will probably never talk to us again. Fuck them. I mean, they are teammates and all that, but we are never going to hang out with them."

"I know. I also got all nervous cause we kept fucking up the snap when you are under center. I don't know why."

"Well Blake gave me some pointers on that. He ate dinner with me tonight," Dakota said.

"Jeez, you are such a natural conversationalist."

"Are you kidding, you can talk the hind leg off a mule," Dakota said in a country twang.

"You're just mocking me like they did."

"No, I'm not. Sorry. Hey, come on. Let's practice something so we are better at the snaps tomorrow. Get down and let me show you."

Bear climbed down from the bed and stood in front of Dakota. "Okay, so what did QB1 tell you we should do?"

Dakota recounted the story Blake had shared with him. Bear listened with a frown and then a smirk sliding across his furry face.

"So, we just need to spend the night with you holding onto my balls and we will be better with the snaps?"

"We just have to get past the awkwardness of it, make it normal. And we have to learn to communicate with me touching your balls so you know what I am going to do."

"It sounds pretty weird to me, but fuck it. I don't want the coach yelling at me tomorrow. I know I may look like an elephant, but I've got pretty thin skin, dude. I struggle with a lot of criticism."

"It's okay, bro. Come on," Dakota tossed Bear a NERF football. He bent over in a crouch and Dakota moved in behind him, his hands sliding firmly against his sack as he set.

Bear looked back at Dakota. "That feels good, baby," he said with a soft hiss.

Dakota punched him softly in the nuts.

"Ooof. Careful bro."

They went through two dozen snaps, Bear clearly feeling the count as Dakota pressed against his sack with the back of his hands. Bear stood up and stretched his back.

"I can still just barely feel what you are doing down there, man."

Dakota stood with his hands on his hips. "Okay. Um, take off your shorts."

"I will if you will," he said fluttering his eyelashes. Dakota pressed his lips together and slid his shorts down to the floor. His cock was hard and jutted his underwear out in a black tent. "Oh shit!" Bear said smiling. He actually reached out and tapped Dakota's erection with a finger. "Okay, you asked for it, man," Bear said sliding his shorts off. He stood in front of his punter, his cock straining against the white cotton fabric of the boxer briefs he was wearing. Dakota smiled and pretended to knock on his roommate's huge boner. Bear pulled back with a giggle before turning around. Dakota walked up and rubbed his hands all over the young man's ass, gripping his round cheeks and sliding his hand down the snapper's crack to his large sack. Bear's balls were egg-sized and hung low in a loose sack. His hand fit easily in-between the large orbs. He stood still and in a moment, could feel Bear's breathing and even his pulse against this hand from the blood flowing in and out of his scrotum.

"I can feel that good. I mean, I can tell where you fingers are and everything," Bear said.

"And if I touch you like this," Dakota said sliding his fingers along his right testicle, it means regular count and snap. If I slide down on the left, it means I am probably going to keep the snap and run with the ball for a fake or quick kick."

"Copy that," Bear said looking at Dakota upside down through his legs with a frown, which Dakota realized was a smile.

"If I grip your sack and lightly squeeze it, it means get ready for a blitz," Dakota said, this time taking his hand and grabbing Bear's balls and gently squeezing them.

"Copy. Hope we get lots of that call," he said smiling wider.

Dakota was amazed at the amount of heat emanating from Bear's ass crack and balls. "You are like a human nuclear reactor, buddy. Your balls are cooking my hands, they are so warm." Dakota ran his fingers up and down his roommate's ass crack. He could feel the furry trench underneath the cotton. He gripped one ball and then the other, and then slid this hand up and around Bear's erection.

"So what signal is that?"

"What?"

"The signal when you grip my cock and jack me?"

Dakota laughed. "I'm just touching you so you get used to having your shit fondled. Blake said it kind of helps get the nerves over with," Dakota said sliding his hand lightly over the big man's genitals, feeling Bear's pulse speed up as his dick grew harder.

"Well, if that's what you want…" Bear said standing up and pushing his shorts down to the floor before bending back over, his furry crack opening up to reveal a dusty brown knot of flesh. His testicles hung low, the left nut lower than the right. Fur lined the crack, the edges of his sack, his balls, and shaft. Dakota took a step back.

"You want me to go under center with you bareass naked?"

"I thought the whole point was to get comfortable," Bear said turning around. His cock was sticking straight out, impossibly long and thick. Bear reached down and gripped Dakota's penis through his shorts and fondled him. "I mean, I never held another guy's junk either. At least, not since I was little kid. Feels fucking hot, in a messed-up sort of way."

Dakota stood still, his legs spread, allowing Bear's hands to manipulate his cock and balls. He slid his thumbs into the elastic of his shorts and pushed his shorts and underwear down to the floor. Bear gripped his naked penis and ran his thumb over the wet tip.

"Fuck. That feels amazing to touch another dick like this. You aren't going to tell anyone, right?"

"No and you better not either," Dakota said. "So turn around and get over that ball."

Bear turned and spread his legs wide, squatting over the NERF ball. His balls hung low and Dakota slid his hand underneath the furry legs and let each one of Bear's balls rest on either side of his hand. He let his fingers slide up and down the man's furry crack, even lightly teasing his asshole that clamped tight and then opened again. He gripped Bear's scrotum and pulled down, again and again, then moved to his dick and did the same.

"It's like you're milking a fucking cow, man. Shit, you better stop or I'm gonna shoot before long."

Dakota stood up, his own penis rock hard and drooling precum. "Well, does it feel a little less strange for me to touch your junk?"

Bear grinned, casually stroking his own penis now. "It felt wicked strange, but fuck, it was pretty fun. And yeah, I think I get it now. Buddy, you can slide hand between my legs and tell me what to do any day. And for what it's worth, it's pretty fucking hot being gay football touchy-feely with you."

Dakota grinned. "I bet Connor would enjoy this practice with you too."

Bear pulled off his t-shirt, now completely naked, like a giant Greek statue.

"You think he likes dick? You think he's a gay?"

"I doubt it, but he enjoys staring at you, like a bunch of the guys do."

"I saw his dick in the shower today. He's hung pretty nice for a smaller guy. He's got tons of tatts and a thick bush. He's uncut though."

"You got a thing about uncut cock?"

"Just never really seen it much before. It is a little strange to me. What about you?"

Dakota gripped his own dick and pulled his foreskin down and over the tip of his penis. "Not really. I mean, I don't know much about it either but sometimes I wonder what it must feel like."

"Hey, I can do that too," Bear said pushing the fat tip of his cock back inside the edges of his trimmed foreskin. "Look at us, anteaters!"

"You are mental," Dakota said shaking his head. Bear looked at him with wild eyes and pounced, tackling the punter and trapping his arms behind his back, pressing him down on the bed. Dakota groaned. "You are gonna crush my chest, you idiot," he hissed through clenched teeth.

"Say you love my big sack."

"No!" Dakota struggled in vain to climb out from under Bear's monstrous weight.

"Say I want to hold them and lick them and make them my toys."

"Gross! I will not!" Dakota said with a laugh. "Oh God, my chest is caving in. Get off me, you ox."

"Say, 'I love Bear and want to pleasure him whenever he wants me to.' Say it!" Bear pushed harder on Dakota's back as he ground his crotch into the punter's backside.

"Ugh. Fine...fine...I love your big sack and I want to hold them and lick them and pleasure you whatever the fuck...just get off!"

Bear rolled off Dakota and patted him on the head. "That's a good boy," he said.

Dakota turned over, laying against Bear on the bed. "You almost crushed me, man. That is going to be killer for some of our opponents."

"Now you know why I got the scholarship."

The guys lay quietly for a minute. Bear reached over and took Dakota's hand and pulled it over and laid it on his swollen dick. Dakota pulled his hand away.

"Fuck! I forgot you are just lying there all sweaty and naked. Jeez, man."

"No point in pretending you don't love it, buddy," Bear said sweetly wrapping Dakota in a bear hug, grinding his naked dick against Dakota's butt.

"Yaaaah! Knock it off, dude!" Dakota pulled away and sat up at the head of his bed, shaking his head at the grinning face of the giant freshman, slowly toying with his cock. "Am I gonna have to fight you off every night?"

Bear rolled over and put his chin on his hands like a baby on a bearskin rug. "Maybe. It's hard to keep my hands to myself."

Dakota climbed down from the bed and popped Bear sharply on his naked, wide ass. "Well, you gotta go easy with me, brother. Remember, I'm still a virgin."

Bear sat up and looked intently at the blond student. "Are you shitting me?"

Dakota smiled and shrugged. "Not shitting you. Pure as the driven snow here."

Bear hopped down from the bed, his furry belly bouncing ever so slightly. "Jesus, man. I thought I was the only guy on the team that still hadn't punched his V-card."

"No fuckin' way!" Dakota said. "For reals?"

"Not bullshitting you, bro. Just never got my dick wet in high school. School was so small, all the girls, they were like sisters. Just seemed too weird. Why didn't you..?"

"Just didn't meet someone I wanted to fuck, I guess. I mean, I went on dates and made out and fooled around some...you know, second-third base stuff."

"Yeah, me too. But the girls I went out with…they couldn't suck dick for shit. Scraped my cock with their teeth all the time."

"Yikes! Yeah, I experienced that too. Just once. You try eating pussy?"

Bear picked up his underwear and shorts and pulled them on. "Yeah. Wasn't a very good experience for me."

"How come?"

"Maybe I just was unlucky, but it kind of smelled and tasted bad to me. Kind of a mix of pee and fish."

"Oh my God. I thought that just happened to me. I really tried to like it, but it was not good."

"I know. And my bro and other guys at school acted like it was the best thing in the whole world. Maybe we just got dud girls to eat out."

"I don't know. I just wasn't into it at all and it made me feel weird and kind of stupid," Dakota said. "My dad told me not to worry about it, that eating pussy wasn't for everyone."

Bear reached out and gripped Dakota by the shoulder. "You talked with your dad about licking pussy? Holy shit! I couldn't do that in a million years. I talked to my bro and he said I was just being a fag and to shut up and try it again."

Dakota frowned. "That's not very nice. Yeah, me and my dad, it's always been good for us to talk about stuff. Pretty much anything I ever wondered about, he and I talked about it."

"You are really lucky to have a Dad like that who is easy to talk with. My pop is so old fashioned and conservative…he pretty much never mentioned sex to me at all other than saying stuff like 'You and your brother need to clean up that room and stop leaving cum rags all over the place. Think of your mother and sister!'"

Dakota laughed.

"And your Dad buys you a fucking sex toy to beat off with for graduation. Yeah, just a bit different. Speaking of Tom Brady...you gonna have another go with him soon?"

"Jeez! Quit calling it that, will you. Yeah, I gotta try it again, maybe with the a-hole attachment this time."

"Mmmm. Will be like fucking Jason Witten or J.J., all tight and smooth and juicy,"

"You are a sick puppy," Dakota said. "Shit, I know it's just 8:00, but I am so tired. You want to do something or...."

"I'm beat too. I'm cool if you want to go to bed. And thanks again for practicing the snaps and everything. I think it really did help," Bear said.

"No prob. Let's just keep the naked part to ourselves, though," Dakota said.

The guys got ready for bed, brushing teeth, flossing, trimming nails and sending off a few texts to friends and family. Dakota checked his phone and had another text from Elmo.

> ➢ Can you meet me over in the north stairwell of Granger Hall tomorrow evening around 7:00 PM?

Dakota typed in his reply:

> ➢ Sure – see you then

Elmo replied:

> ➢ Hold on to your cornhole with that big Bear of yours. L8tr. E.

Dakota answered

> ➢ He might need to watch out for his. :-o D

Dakota stood in front of the toilet and exhaled, sending a loud, long piss into the bowl. Bear followed him in and stood to the side of the john and pulled out his dick, making huge bubbles in the bright white toilet.

"You gonna come in here every time I need to wiz, man?"

"Nah, but it's cool, right?"

Dakota rolled his eyes and patted Bear on the shoulder. "Yah, it's all good. Don't forget to flush that shit."

The players lay in the dark, quiet of their room. Fans hummed above their heads and the soft, occasional slamming of doors or laughter in the hallways filled the air. Bear tossed and turned, fidgeting in the bed trying to get comfortable, his big feet and legs whacking Dakota's in the shins and knees as he did.

"Hey, kicky! Knock it off, will ya?"

"I can't get comfortable. I need to relax. You got any weed?" Bear asked.

"Um, no. And you can't do weed and be on the football team, you know that."

"It's so stupid to live in a state where pot is legal and you can't even enjoy it."

"Word! Maybe you should try meditation or something."

"Maybe you should try blowing me," Bear snapped back.

The guys continued to struggle with falling asleep, changing positions and turning over back and forth. Finally Dakota sat up.

"You want to fuck Tom Brady? Would that help you get to sleep?"

"It's only Tom Brady if you use the mouth. If it's the asshole, it's Jason Witten or J.J. So smooth..!"

"Sure, whatever," Dakota leaned over and pulled the fleshlight out of his drawer. He swapped out the opening and screwed on the butthole attachment. He slid his finger inside. It was super tight and smooth. He grabbed the bottle of lube and laid it in between the players' beds pushed together.

"Okay then. There you go. But I get to watch this time," Dakota said grinning.

Bear raised his ass off the bed and pushed down his underwear. His cock was soft and laid on his furry belly, his big ballsack rolling between his muscled thighs.

"Okay with me, bro. You gonna lube me up?"

"I think you can do that."

"Well that's no fun," the big furry freshman said tipping a generous supply of Gun Oil into his palm and slathering it on his penis. Bear's cock grew hard in just a few moments. He picked up the sex toy and laid the anal opening against the head of his penis and pushed inside, his eyes closing to slits with a low moan rumbling from his throat.

"Holy God! You didn't say it felt that good, brother," Bear said forcing his huge cock deep into the toy until the pink vinyl lay against his massive balls, buried in his dark black crop of pubes. Dakota slid his hand inside his shorts as he watched his roommate pump his big cock in and out of the toy.

"Oh Jesus. Yeah, oh yeah. Take that cock, Jason. Mmmm, feel it right up against your prostate, bro. How does that feel? Got way more meat in your than when Romo fucks your hole. I bet Dak has pumped a few loads into your smooth tight end, bro. Oh yeah, spread that wide ass for me and take that cock..!" Bear muttered and continued to pump the toy up and down on his massive erection.

"Jesus, Bear..." Dakota whispered watching the freshman destroy the tight asshole toy. It made a soft sucking, squishing sound as he pumped it back and forth.

"Take that, dick, 82. Oh yeah, bend over and let me breed you, bro. Let me add my nut to all that jizz Romo and Dak have pumped up your wide ass. Oh fuck! I'm gonna cum!"

Bear bounced his big ass up and down off the mattress, holding the Fleshlight with both hands. He threw his head back and jammed his cock as deep as possible inside. Dakota watched his bull balls rolling and contracting in the loose sack, pumping blast after blast of hot nut into the toy until a tiny river of white began to leak from the stretched ring around Bear's penis. He fell back, exhausted. His erection holding the toy up in the air, bobbing back and forth along with his balls every time he clinched his asshole and sent more juice into the sleeve. Dakota's cock was cock hard now and in his hand. Bear raised his head up, and then slid the toy off his dick. His penis was fat and wet and streaked with sperm. He lifted himself on one elbow and took the stretched opening of the toy and pushed until Dakota's dick slid inside.

"Oh shit! It's all warm and wet and cummy. Fuck!" Dakota said taking the handle of the toy and pumping it back and forth on his penis, jamming as far inside as he could. His balls rolled to the side, tight and round in his smooth sack. The blond pubes around the opening looked like soft rolls of honeyed cotton.

"Do it, bud. Fuck that tight end. Fill him up again. Mix your nut with me and Dak and Romo. Oh yeah, he's bent over and taking all your spunk, dude. Fuck that hole!"

Dakota shouted, "Uhhhhng!" and unloaded his testicles deep into the toy already filled with Bear's load. Dakota and Bear's mixed semen flowed out the edges of the toy and pooled in the soft fur around Dakota's cock as the boy lay exhausted and spent.

The freshmen laid in silence, the fans cooling them off, as sweat dripped from their faces. The room was dark other than the light from Dakota's laptop bathing both of them in blue. Dakota slid the toy from his cock and let it drop to the floor. His mind reeled. He had just experienced the most amazing, intense orgasm of his life with a fucking plastic tube and a furry man lying beside him. He was conflicted, embarrassed, and trembling with post-release euphoria. He could hear Bear's breathing heavy and hard beside him, slowing down with his own to regular breaths. Dakota smiled as he felt Bear's large hand slide round his own and squeeze tight.

"Hands down. The best cum I ever had," Bear whispered, his large thumb softy caressing Dakota's hand.

"Me too, bro. Jeez, all that nut squishing around my dick in the Fleshlight – mixing my cum with yours, Damn!" Dakota said, lightly squeezing the snapper's huge hand.

The fans droned and sent a stead breeze over their chests, evaporating the few drops of sweat. "Kinda gay, I guess, but fuck. So fun too," Bear said. His face was inches away from Dakota's as they lay on their pillows. Dakota's fingers traced along the furry knuckles gripping his hand. He had never held a guy's hand in his whole life, at least not like this. His mind and thoughts spun in circles as his dick swelled fat again.

"I don't care if it was gay. It's nobody's business. I just can't believe how good..."

"I know, man. Same for me. So, you think it's just because we are horned up, or because it was sorta dirty and gay sexy and all that, or..."

"Or maybe 'cause it was us doing it, not somebody else? Yeah, fuck if I know," Dakota. "But I don't know that I could have done that with anybody else?"

"Not even Elmo?"

"What?"

"I kinda looked at your phone, man. Sorry. I didn't mean to, I just looked to see who was texting you so much."

Dakota looked at Bear, annoyed but just shook his head. "I don't really care about him."

"I hear you. Cool that he's into dick, though. I mean, it's pretty brave still to be all out and proud on a football team."

"I don't think anyone else knows he is interested in guys. And not our place to tell guys."

Bear squeezed Dakota's hand again. "No worries, man. Not our business. I mean, unless he tries to move in and make you his little bitch. I might have a problem with that."

Dakota laughed. "His little bitch, huh? Maybe he would be my little bitch."

"Probably more like it. What do you call those gay boys who enjoy taking it up the ass?"

"Um, a bottom?"

"Yeah, that's right. Bottom. What about you? If you are gonna ever go gay, would you be the bottom or top guy?"

Dakota's eyes narrowed and he looked intently at Bear. "Who the fuck knows, man? I think some guys like it both ways anyway?"

"Really? What do they call themselves?"

"I think it's versatile or vers."

"Okay. Well cool. In my gay fantasy, I will be vers." Bear said leaning his head over so that it touched Dakota's.

"You are full of shit, you know that, right?"

"My bro's been telling me that since I was like eight. You ready to try and sleep?"

"Sure, I'll try. My mind's pretty freaked out right now."

Bear turned on his side and pulled Dakota over, spooning around him with his thick furry legs, his big hands rubbing on Dakota's smooth belly. "Oh shit, well me too, buddy. I don't know what the fuck is going on with me but I just want to tell you one thing."

"What's that, Baloo?"

"Baloo?"

"The big bear from The Jungle Book movie," Dakota explained.

"Oh yeah. Coolio. Well, anyway…" the large freshman wrapped himself tighter around Dakota, his lips and mustache tickling the blond boy's ear as he whispered.

"I don't know what the fuck all this is, but I would rather be here figuring it out with you than anyone else in the world. I know we just met and all that, but damn, it feels like we have known each other forever."

Dakota reached up and touched the side of Bear's furry face with his hand. "You got that right, brother. If I'm gonna be half-gay sharing a fucking Fleshlight, sticking my dick in a big puddle of someone's spooge…I'd rather it be you than anyone else."

Bear leaned forward and gave Dakota a loud, wet smack on the side of the face. "Thanks for being my BF."

Dakota looked back at him suspiciously. "Boyfriend?"

"Best friend! But, I'll take boyfriend too. As long as that's between us." Night brother."

7. First Game

School took off with a blast and kicked both Dakota and Bear's ass in the first week. Every class seemed to have so much homework, labs, and reading and football practice was insane. Every night, the guys barely made it back to their room before collapsing in front of their desks and studying until they climbed into bed, too tired to hardly move. The players would lay in bed and talk about the day, run through plays or talk about the upcoming game against Puget Sound University. Dakota had to admit, lying in bed beside his roomie, this big, furry, sweaty, cuddly goofball was the highlight of his day. Inevitably, as they were getting quiet and falling asleep, Bear would either wrap himself around Dakota and hold him tight or reach over to grasp his hand. That contact made Dakota's heart swell almost as much as his dick.

More than once, he had woken to find his roomie spooned close behind him, his huge cock speared into his ass crack, rubbing on his underwear as his large hands rubbed his chest or belly. Twice now, he had laid there and quietly stroked his cock, soaking in the warmth and closeness, spilling his seed into his hand. Dakota had never been one to taste his own semen, but lying there with Bear all wrapped around him, he did. He tipped the contents of his palm into his mouth and licked his hand clean. He found himself thinking more and more about dick every day.

His punting had been getting steadily better, mostly due to the tight connection between he and Bear. The coach had patted both of them on the ass multiple times telling other members of the special teams unit that was the way he expected all of them to connect and read each other's minds. More than one of the guys had joked with them that their butt love must be giving them the edge, and for some reason, Bear just laughed and went along with it like it was the truth, grabbing and hugging Dakota in front of them all the time like they were a real couple. Dakota acted the part of the reluctant and slightly annoyed participant, but secretly, he loved every minute of it. He saw the way Connor, DaQuan, and LaDarius stared at them in the showers, standing close and being way more conversant than they had been at first.

But the real surprise, of course, had been Elmo. Since the texts and photos they had shared, Dakota had put off meeting up with Elmo as he had suggested. He just didn't know if he was ready to cross that line yet. But he had to admit, the sexy banter and the small red-head back standing naked next to him in the shower was beginning to have a big effect on him. Elmo had a perfect ass, round, big, and lightly dusted with honey red fuzz. His cock was about six inches, but thick and round and hung beautifully across his full sack.

On Wednesday evening of the first week of class, Dakota was feeling totally burned out and wanted a coffee and a walk to clear his head. Bear was in a late lab. Dakota left the room and walked down to Dutch Bros for a large frozen Carmelizer. He was walking back through the City Park when his phone buzzed. Dakota looked at the screen. The text was from Elmo.

> - You are here at the park?
> - Yeah. U?
> - Come in the bathroom
> - WTF? Now?
> - Now

Dakota looked up and saw the rest room on the edge of the park. It was a brand new structure that went along with the new bandstand that had been built in the summer. He opened the door to the bathroom and saw it was empty. As he stood in the doorway, he heard a small cough from the back stall. Dakota walked to the back of the bathroom and the stall door slowly opened. Elmo stood inside, his shorts down around his ankles, slowly stroking his erect cock. Dakota stood open-mouthed and staring, looking back at the door and then around the stall. He moved up and closed and locked the stall. He took the drink from Dakota and placed it on the toilet paper dispenser. He sat on the toilet and reached out and began to stroke Dakota's cock through his shorts. He reached inside and pulled out the punter's hard penis and swallowed it balls deep in one gulp. Dakota's head slid back, his eyes closed. He gripped Elmo's short red curls and force-fed him every inch of his boner, skull-fucking him until saliva ran down his chin and choking grunts filled the stall. Dakota's balls mashed hard against the running back's face as Elmo's hands gripped Dakota's round ass, pulling him further and further into his hungry mouth.

Then, just as Dakota was getting close to exploding, Elmo stopped sucking. He pulled out a foil condom package and ripped it open and slid it onto Dakota's firm erection. The running back turned around and presented his furry ass. His hole was wet and sticky, obviously lubed.

"Okay bro. Get that big dick in my pussy. Fuckin' take my cherry."

Dakota stared but stepped forward and pointed his large dick head into Elmo's pulsing hole. He pushed forward three times before the tight sphincter relaxed and opened enough for his large cock to slide inside. The boy groaned and bent lower as Dakota plowed all seven inches of his penis inside his tight hole. Dakota held still for a moment, and then proceeded to bang the hell out of the freshman. The concrete walls of the stall echoed with the slaps, smacks, and grunts from Dakota's relentless fuck. He pounded the boy for a minute and felt his orgasm ready to explode.

"I'm gonna nut," Dakota whispered.

Elmo pulled Dakota's cock from his ass and fell to his knees, ripping off the rubber and sucking him deep as his semen blasted into the running back's gulping mouth. Dakota groaned and unloaded his balls into the red-head's eager face. Elmo stood and moved close to Dakota and pressed his mouth to the punter's. His tongue slid inside with half of Dakota's load still held there. Dakota freaked out, but held it together, tasting his own sperm and his teammate's warm tongue.

"Shit man, I have wanted to do that since the minute I first saw you," Elmo whispered.

"Really?"

"Yeah. I figured you and Bear were already…"

"Nah, man. That was a first for me."

"Holy shit. I been sucking dick since I was a freshman in high school. What did you think?"

"I don't know. Still in shock. But it was fucking hot for sure."

"Think you might want to try it again sometime?"

Dakota pushed his dick back into his shorts and grabbed his coffee, taking a drink to rinse away the sperm flavor in his mouth. "Maybe, but honestly…that was pretty intense. I don't really think I'm gay or anything."

"Shit man, who said anything about that. I just want to get off and have fun and don't have time for a girlfriend, even though I don't think I really like girls that much." Elmo pulled up his shorts and reached over to slowly rub and stroke Dakota's still hard dick. "Every time I see you...and Bear too for that matter, I just want you both to fuck the shit out of me. I'm probably fucking gay, but whatever...I just want to have fun."

Dakota smiled. "I hear you, bro. But next time, let's maybe go for another place other than a public bathroom. It's fucking sexy, but too risky for me. I need to run."

Dakota turned to leave and Elmo caught him by the hand. "Don't tell anyone. Okay?"

Dakota smiled and squeezed the short guy's hand. "No worries there, buddy. Our secret."

Dakota had almost told Bear about the adventure with Elmo several times, but held back for some reason. He had the distinct feeling that Bear would act all cool about it, but down deep, might be either weirded out by it or even a bit jealous. Dakota totally rationalized the entire thing, telling himself that he was indeed, still a virgin, since he had used a condom and it was just a random quickie. He knew it might be bullshit, but it was the way he felt, so fuck it.

Bear continued to want to practice under-center handoffs almost every night before they went to bed. Dakota now felt totally at home under the big freshman's spread legs, resting his hands on the snapper's huge balls to hike the ball. In fact, there was something so fun and comforting about it, Dakota would rub and tease Bear's testicles in addition to running through the various scenarios for gadget plays. If Dakota ever tried to short cut the practice, Bear would turn around and glare at his roomie with a withering stare, until Dakota's hands slid underneath him.

The team's first game of the year was a road trip, against the Loggers of Puget Sound. Dakota found himself growing more and more nervous and uptight as the game grew nearer. He could tell Bear felt the same, as did Connor, Elmo, and the others. The upperclassmen seemed to have it all together, but even they seemed less carefree and more focused. The guys would be boarding a bus for the five hour ride on Friday morning. For some reason, Dakota had been paired with Connor Tuafila as his on-the-road roommate for this game with Bear being paired up with Elmo Fonda of all things. As soon as Dakota heard this, he found himself nervous and wondering if he should tell Bear about the encounter in the bathroom. There was also this strange, new sensation that he could almost call jealousy, which was ridiculous.

The night before they boarded the bus, after their ritual of working through the snaps, Bear was sitting on the john playing some game while Dakota shaved. Bear's big furry legs were so long, they filled up the small bathroom. Lucky for Dakota, the big guy's dump was uncharacteristically decent tonight, so he wasn't rushing to close the door to keep the smell from the rest of the room. He walked up to Bear, his face still half covered with shaving cream.

"Damn, I wish we were rooming together tomorrow night up in Tacoma."

Bear looked up with a frown furrowed across his forehead. "That makes two of us, bro-seph. It's fucked up for sure. How am I supposed to keep calm and get a good sleep without my Cuddle Koda beside me?"

"And my big furry Baloo, rubbing his boner up my crack in the middle of the night."

Bear laughed. "Dude, I don't do that."

"The fuck you don't, man."

Bear put his phone down on the back of the toilet. He had changed from the game and photos from his Tumblr were on the screen: a large furry guy with his face buried deep in a smooth guy's round ass. "Seriously? I really rub my D in your crack when we sleep?"

Dakota smiled. "Well, you seem pretty dead asleep but yeah, you give me a boner burn some nights."

Bear wiped his ass and flushed. His face was several shades pinker than normal. "Man, I'm sorry about that. I remember my bro back home would sometimes rub and grope me in his sleep when we were growing up. Sorry if it's upsetting you." The big man looked contrite and more like a little boy than Dakota had ever seen him. The punter stepped close and playfully gripped the guy's cock through his shorts.

"I don't mind, Baloo. In fact, it's kinda cool. I don't know if I'd be so agreeable if it were, say...Elmo or Dillon, but with you. No problem."

Bear smiled and gave Dakota's sack a light squeeze. "Hey, you missed a little of your whiskers there, furry boy," he said sarcastically, running a thick finger through the shaving cream. Dakota laughed.

"Hey, don't go rubbing up on ole Elmo tomorrow night. That's my gig. You and him find some other way to get off together."

"Har, har, roomie. That red-headed little squirt couldn't handle all this awesomeness," he said holding his arms out. His thick, furry chest was a carpet that continued all the way into the waistband of his briefs, which were round and bulging in front. Dakota smiled but in the back of his mind, he figured Elmo would want nothing better than to try.

As the two lay in bed that night, Dakota edged his butt over to the middle of the joined beds, but found that Bear was facing the other direction. Dakota turned over and spooned up close behind Bear, sliding an arm around to his furry belly.

"Dang, Koda. You extra horned up tonight, or what?"

Dakota instantly felt embarrassed and slightly annoyed. He patted Bear on the arm and turned over to try and sleep. Unseen to Dakota, Bear stared at the wall, a single tear sliding from his eye.

The following morning, Bear and Dakota sat quietly together in the bus, headphones on. Their legs were pressed together due to the seats being rather small. The two had not said more than a half-dozen words that morning. Dakota was half mad, half sad and altogether miserable as they drove up I5 toward Tacoma. The day was overcast and the inside of the tinted windowed bus was quite dark. Dakota closed his eyes and tried to nap, trying to concentrate on anything to make him feel more positive. At some point, Bear must have taken his hoodie off and laid it across his lap. Dakota roused when he felt the man's large hand grip his own. Dakota looked up in surprise and slight terror, but realized, their hands were hidden under the hoodie. Bear's big thumb slowly caressed Dakota's hand as they drove along. Dakota let his head slid over and rest on the big guy's shoulder, noticing that the guys across from them were sleeping away as well. Bear whispered.

"Sorry for being a dick, brother," he said in a very low voice.

Dakota squeezed his hand. "Me too, bro."

"I'm gonna miss you tonight. First time I haven't had your sweet ass there beside me to rub against in the middle of the night."

"I know, Bear. I'm gonna miss it too."

"You're my good luck charm, bro-ski."

Dakota squeezed Bear's hand. "You're mine, too, brutha-dent."

"Don't fuck around with Connor too much tonight, okay. Save it for me," Bear said even lower into Dakota's ear.

"I won't. And don't let Elmo turn you into his bitch either." Dakota instantly felt guilty about the stupid hook-up in the park bathroom. He just couldn't admit that to Bear right now.

"Dude, like he even could. I might abuse him a little...you can do the same with Connor."

Dakota laughed. "Maybe I will. So how far can I go?"

Bear made a hmmm sound. "Not sure, but no one gets your V-card buddy before me."

"Who said I was a virgin?"

"Yeah right," Bear laughed softly, squeezing Dakota's hand again.

"Well then, your big V-card hole is mine too."

"You honestly think I am still cherry, bro?"

Dakota pressed his lips against Bear's ear. "I know your manhole is – I don't care how many skank hoes you fucked. It doesn't count."

"Exactly zero like I told you." Bear grinned, moving his hand over and clandestinely squeezing Dakota's penis. "Okay, my man. My pussy is all yours," he said in a whisper out of the side of his mouth. He continued to massage Dakota's dick until he had a raging boner.

"Thanks for that, Bear. Now what am I gonna do?"

"Just helping you keep your edge, Punter."

The team arrived in Tacoma around 3:00 PM. It only took about twenty minutes for the team to get checked in and find their rooms. Bear gave Dakota a big pouty frown as he headed off to find his room. Dakota found an elevator and went up to the sixth floor and found room 604. Connor was already in the room, plugging in his iPad to a plug.

"Hey Dakota. You care which side, man?"

"Nah. This one's fine though," Dakota said laying his duffle bag on the bed closest to the door. He pulled a few things out of his bag including his small clip-on fan and started looking for a place to attach it and plug it in.

"I should have known you were just like me. Look, I'm your biggest fan!" Connor said holding up a small fan of his own. Dakota reached out and fist-bumped the Hawaiian kicker.

"Yeah, Bear and I have two of these going in our room. IT's like a wind tunnel in there at night. But it covers up his snoring."

"Oh tell me about it. Elmo snores like a buzz saw. I wear earplugs sometimes, brah. Did you think it was weird, them mixing us up like this instead of just letting us stay with our regular dorm roommates?"

"Yeah," Dakota said pulling out more things from his duffle bag and throwing in a dresser drawer. "Bear was pretty pissed...I think I'm like a security blanket for him or something. I know he's this huge monster, but he's kind of a sweet, gentle soul really."

"Hey man, I can sense that. It's why he's cool to be around. I can't figure Elmo out half the time. Sometimes, he seems very chill and other times like he's got a deep dark secret, like he's a serial killer or something. "

Dakota laughed. "I can see that, though I doubt he is the Dexter type guy really." Dakota reached into his duffle bag and found another shirt. He pulled it out. As he did, the shirt unrolled and the object hidden inside flew across the room and landed in the middle of Connor's bed. The guys stared in mute horror.

It was the fucking Fleshlight! Dakota closed his eyes and bit his lip. Connor picked up the fat tube and held it, his eyes growing wide. The place kicker touched the soft vinyl lips of the tube and burst into a loud, low laugh.

"Goddamn it, Bear! I am going to kill him." Dakota reached for the toy but Connor held it away from him.

"Wait just a minute, brah. Damn, you come prepared like a boy scout for sure. Holy shit, man. That's either really brave or really messed up to bring your sex toy along on an away game. Is it like your lucky charm or something?"

Dakota tackled the smaller guy and tried to wrestle away the Fleshlight. Connor kept switching hands with it, laughing like a hyena. Dakota fattened him on the bed and gripped his arm, but the toy was just out of reach. Dakota clinched his teeth, trying not to laugh or scream. And in the middle of all this, he could tell his fucking cock was growing hard, rubbing against Connor's as they thrashed about on the bed. Finally, he relented and rolled off the kicker, allowing the man to study and touch the soft lips of the toy. As he slid his finger inside the mouth, his own mouth opened in a sensual O.

"Jesus Christ, that feels way too real, man. These lips...they look like someone to me."

Dakota lay back on the bed, covering his eyes with his hands. "Tom Brady."

"What?"

"Bear says the lips look like Tom Brady."

Connor studied the toy for a moment more. "Shit, you're right. Damn, that's messed up to be getting sucked off by Tom Brady. But whatever floats your boat, brah. Where did you get this thing?"

Dakota took it from Connor's hand. "It was a graduation gift...a gag gift, from my dad."

"Holy shit, dude. That is crazy. My dad would be way too hung up and embarrassed to give this to me. Fuck, he never mentioned one word about sex or puberty or anything to me growing up. I learned everything from my bro and guys at school."

Dakota sat up and slid his own finger into the lips of the toy, not having any fucks left to give. "Yeah, me and my dad, we are pretty close with shit like that. It's good most of the time. Sometimes, like this, it can be a bit much."

"You use it yet?" Connor asked. Dakota watched as the kicker adjusted his growing bulge in his shorts.

Dakota laughed. "Hell yeah. It's the real deal as far as jack off toys go."

"I take it Bear stuck that in the bag to bust your balls."

"Got that right. I'll get him for sure. I think I'll fill the fucker with Ben-Gay...then the next time he slides his sausage inside...he'll get a warm welcome."

Connor roared. Then he abruptly sat up and stared. "Hold it, man. Next time...you mean, he's stuck his big cock in your toy thing? Oh man, that's sick. And kind of hot."

Dakota rolled over on his belly and proceeded to tell Connor about the first day when Bear walked in on him and the Fleshlight. The kicker's laughter was so loud, someone on the other side of the wall pounded on it to quiet them down.

"You are gonna get us fucking busted," Dakota said.

"Oh man, that is so rich. Hey…Elmo has walked in on me twice, man. But I didn't have such a cool toy to play with. And I walked in on him once in the shower, with him stroking off and his other hand buried knuckle deep in his butt hole."

"Oh shit!" Dakota said giggling along with Connor. The guys lay on the beds and let the funny moments wind down, with Dakota still fingering the lips of the toy."

"Okay, that is creeping me out now cause you are right, it is fucking Tom Brady's mouth, sucking on your finger there." Conner sat up, his penis now at full alert tenting out his shorts. He leaned closer. "So roomie…do I get a turn with that fucker tonight?"

Dakota threw the Fleshlight at Connor's head, barely missing him. "You might as well start now, dude. You are already boned up. Slide your meat inside, man."

"I was hoping for a little privacy for me and ole Tom here."

"No fucking way. I get to watch, that's the deal."

Connor laughed. "Okay brah. You want to see me beat off, I can accommodate that. So you and Bear take turns with this thing? You do sloppy seconds after his big nut goes off inside?"

Dakota didn't say a word which made Connor roar with laughter again, eliciting another pounding on the walls. "Oh shit, man. You do! That is so sick. We gotta try that tonight. Hey, we better go down for dinner. I am gonna be thinking of the two of you cumming in that toy all night long."

The guys entered the banquet hall and went through the buffet line. They found Bear and Elmo already sitting at a table and joined them. Bear seemed his usual happy self, but underneath, Dakota could sense he was not a happy camper. And he for sure didn't care for the joking camaraderie that seemed to be percolating between Dakota and Connor. When Connor got up to get some hot sauce for his Mexican food, Bear leaned over to the punter.

"Shit, you guys already boning each other? Sure seem all happy as crap right now," Bear hissed.

Dakota swallowed. "Calm down, sweetheart. I only let him put the tip in. I am still your boo." Elmo must have overheard because he began to laugh and then choke on his food. Bear had to slap him hard on the back to get it back up.

"I'm gonna Heimlich the shit out of you, Elmo. Calm the fuck down," Bear barked. Dakota roared again.

The players finished dinner and decided to hit the pool and hot tube before turning in for the night. It was mandatory lights out for the players at 9:30 since the call time in the morning was breakfast at 6:30 AM. Dakota waved goodbye to Bear from the elevator, gripping his cock and shaking it tauntingly as the doors closed, with Bear shoving a big middle finger up in Dakota's face. I am gonna pay for that next week, he thought. But he was loving the playful meanness of the whole situation. Dakota and Connor dug through their stuff and found swim trunks. Dakota smirked as he saw Connor staring at his naked ass in the mirror of the room. Dakota tossed his suit on the bed and walked naked to the bathroom and took a loud piss. He came back to see Connor bent over, his loose, floppy balls hanging down low between his legs as he stepped into his board shorts, his round tanned ass smooth and muscular. He turned around and his penis was clearly outlined in the thin shorts.

"I don't know, Brah. Something about hanging out with you is making my pecker do a happy dance."

"Yeah, I have that effect on everyone!"

They rode down in the elevator and found the party in full swing in the indoor pool. There were big beefy football players everywhere. The few little boys that were in the pool to start with ran off when they saw all the giant guys crowding into the pool. It was loud and raucous, with music playing and guys splashing, laughing, playing water basketball and soaking in the hot tub. At one point, the entire O-Line emerged from the dressing room wearing nothing but thong Speedos and proceeded to pose and moon the entire team, eliciting hoots of pleasure and snorts of laughter from the guys. The large players were solid muscle and had big round asses that were somehow way more indecent in the thong than naked in the locker room. Every one of them had a big round basket, their cocks clearly defined in the thin fabric. As they got in the water, more than one of the defensive tackles came up behind them and did the dry hump thing, which was funny and caused a huge wave of water to splash around the pool.

Dakota saw Bear and Elmo come in and he navigated through the shallow end of the pool over to where he was standing and casually let his hand slide in between the big guy's legs in a teasing poke. Bear looked annoyed at first, pulling away from Dakota's hand. When Dakota gave him a WTF expression, Bear grabbed him in a big hug and pulled him under water. Bear's hand slid all the way inside Dakota's suit and fondled his dick as they thrashed about under the water. Dakota opened his eyes and grinned at Bear who was smiling himself. The long snapper's finger moved close to the punter's asshole and almost went inside. Bear mouthed the words..."All Mine," before letting Dakota go. They surfaced and Bear hugged his roommate, rubbing his head.

"Gonna be a great game tomorrow, bro," Bear said.

"Yeah. Gonna rock, brother. You and Elmo get cozy yet?"

Bear looked over at the redhaired back chatting with some other players and rolled his eyes. "That guy is whack...but we've had a couple of laughs. I'll fuck him for good luck or something tonight."

"Oh really? What about your V-card?"

"My butthole is all yours, man. You know that. Just make sure yours remains mine too," Bear said, his hand gripping Dakota's ass and tickling his anus. Dakota nervously looked around but saw no one was paying attention.

"It's all yours...but quit making me wait so long, man" Dakota whispered swimming away.

The coaching staff told the players to get out of the pool around 8:30 and everyone obeyed. The O-Line guys tried to wrap towels around themselves, but they were so tiny, they just gave up and proudly walked back to their rooms with their bare asses showing. Dakota wondered if some of the guests snapping photos with their phones were going to post the pics online. He figured that would create some sort of drama for later.

Dakota and Connor made it back to their room and took off their swim trunks. Connor stepped into the shower to rinse off the chlorine.

"Hey, you want me to just leave the water going?" He said as he was soaping up his hair. Dakota was taking a long piss and said yes.

"Well come on and get in, man. You can wash my back for me," Connor said with a grin, raising up his eyebrows twice as he waited.

"That's a pretty small shower, dude...but okay," Dakota said stepping into the tub. He was standing belly to belly with the Hawaiian kicker. Connor ran the soap over Dakota's shoulders and down his chest before turning him around and washing off his back.

"In Hawaii, men and boys wash one another like this all the time. It's like a ritual," Connor said sliding the slick soap down Dakota's smooth, strong back toward the top of his ass crack. The kickers strong hand held on to Dakota's shoulder while his other rubbed the soap back and forth across Dakota, slipping under his armpits to lather up the hair there and around to his belly, soaping up his furry trail on his belly. Dakota closed his eyes, enjoying the firm hand rubbing against him. He stepped back and felt Connor's erection bump into his butt cheeks. He moved his hand back and gripped Connor's cock.

"Do the Hawaiian dads get all boned up like this washing their boys?"

"Mine always did," Connor said reaching around and grasping Dakota's seven-inch dick. "Shit, man...you and Bear got big dicks, brah."

"Yours is plenty big and thicker than mine too," Dakota said enjoying how Connor's fat cock slid back and forth in his fist. The kicker's foreskin was short and the wide, round head of his penis was already peeking out. "You're like the first uncut guy I ever really looked at."

"Really? Yeah, I guess most of the guys on the team are clipped. What do you think?"

"Feels cool to slide the skin back and all that. Bet it feels good to you."

Connor stepped closer, his face right against Dakota's, continuing to jack his cock back and forth. "It would feel even better sliding in your tight, pussy, brah." Connor moved his penis until the tip was resting inside Dakota's soapy crack, rubbing against his tender hole. "Let me put it in, man. I'll go easy."

Dakota's heart was beating fast. The idea of Connor's cock sliding inside him actually sounded amazing. But as the kicker pushed a bit more, pressing hard against his rosebud, Bear's big furry face and wide grin appeared in his mind. He pulled away.

"I don't know if I'm ready for that, bro. Feels great, all this touching and teasing, but I never got fucked before." Dakota spun around, his own erection rubbing against the kicker's now. "Maybe we could start slower," he said. He saw tiny water droplets on Connor's thick long black lashes, his face very close. His lips were inches from the kicker's soft black mustache. His hand slid back and forth between his erection and his loose sack, rolling the kicker's testicles between his fingers.

"You ever sucked a cock before, brah?"

Dakota shook his head. "How about you?"

"A few times. You want to get out and do a sixty-nine...you know, for luck tomorrow? I did that last year with our former punter. Kyle Williams, he and I were always on-the-road roommates."

Dakota's soapy fingers disappeared into the soft brown cheeks of Connor's ass crack, easily slipping inside his tight hole. The kicker spread his legs to let Dakota's fingers in deeper. The kicker's thick digits pressed against Dakota's sphincter and penetrated him to the first knuckle. Dakota sighed.

"Shit, man. Let's get out of here and blow each other before I let you rape my ass."

Connor smiled. "You can't rape the willing, brah. You saving your pussy for Bear?"

"Something like that...maybe."

"That's cool. I saved mine for a good bud as well."

"Who was that?"

"My pastor's son. We fucked like there was no tomorrow, man."

"That's hot. You just like guys or..."

"No need to be picky, you know. Lots of love to go around," he said. "Gotta live Aloha, you know?"

"Mahalo. Let's get out of here before I blow a nut," Dakota said.

The players turned off the shower and dried off, helping one another with their back and ass. Dakota followed Connor's round tan ass to his bed and climbed in beside him. Connor spun around so that his face was down around Dakota's knees. "Shit, dude. Your dick is big from down here." He casually gripped Dakota's penis and stuck out his tongue to taste the drip of precum on the tip. "Love that honey. That stuff tastes the best."

Dakota sucked in his breath, relishing the touch of the kicker's tongue on his dick head. He held Connor's cock, sliding the extra skin back to expose the wide brown tip. He had wondered about this for so long, came so close with a couple of friends before. But here it was, a fat hard dripping cock right in front of his nose. He could smell the soap and musk wafting from the folds of skin. He opened his mouth and felt the rigid tube slide inside until Connor's tidy black bush tickled his nose. He pulled back slightly to allow his gag reflex to relax, then pushed his nose back into the soft fur and began to suck in a steady rhythm that matched Connor's slow action on his cock. The kicker was masterful, using his tongue and lips, bathing his balls with his tongue before going back to suck Dakota's thick shaft, pulling him tight into his face.

Dakota's mind was racing. He was full of passion and lust, then part of him was recoiling from what he was actually doing. He looked up, Connor's heavy balls were there. He opened his mouth and took one orb into his tongue, swirling it around. He pushed his face further into Connor's crotch until he was looking at the kicker's furry ass crack. He moved his face closer and stuck out his tongue to taste the sophomore's tender brown knuckle of flesh. Below, he felt Connor's face mash into his own crack, lapping and sucking on his asshole while he jacked Dakota's cock. The sensations were almost too much.

"Brah, I'm gonna blow in just a minute," Connor warned. Dakota slid the kicker's fat cock back into his mouth and began to suck and suck and suck until the Hawaiian penis in his mouth swelled and blasted out thick creamy loads of semen into Dakota's surprised mouth. The taste was bitter and sour, not really Dakota's favorite, but he swallowed and licked the nut off the kicker's dick all the same. Then, just as he was cleaning off another drip of sperm, he felt his own orgasm erupt, filling the kicker's mouth with his huge load, dumping his nuts into the lapping mouth. The players continued to suck and lick one another until their penises began to grow hard again. Connor reached down and pulled Dakota up to his face and held him tightly as their let their crotches grind together.

"That's some good luck for sure, brah. Fuck, you almost drowned me with all that nut."

"You too. First time I ever tasted a guy's spunk."

"What'd you think?"

"Tastes like chicken." The guys laughed, then Dakota added. "Kinda tastes like shit. But it's fucking hot, man."

"Sure it, brah. Swallowing some special team sperm...that's our lucky charm, man. Gotta have that nut and we will win for sure.

Dakota lay back on the pillow, enjoying the gentle touches from Connor to his belly and dick as they cuddled on his bed.

"Wonder if ole Bear is gonna get some good luck himself," he whispered.

"If I know Elmo...I bet he does."

Upstairs in room 812, Bear was washing his pits in the shower when the curtain pulled back to reveal a naked Elmo standing in the bathroom, his six inch cock hard and pointed to the sky. Bear looked at the running back and smirked.

"What's up, dude? I mean, other than your cock?"

"You want to drop a load in my mouth or ass, man? Take the edge off before the game tomorrow?"

Bear ran the soap around his rapidly swelling penis. "That sounds okay to me, dude. You sure about it?"

The small player stepped into the tub and pulled the curtain back. He wrapped his arms as far around Bear as he could, his hands gripping the man's hairy ass, his face pressed into the long snapper's furry chest.

"I'll do anything you say, sir. Make me your little bitch," he whispered.

Bear looked down at the bright copper hair and gripped a round ass cheek in each hand. "Okay, you little turd. Get down there and munch on my furry hole, dude." Bear pushed Elmo to the floor of the tub and spread his legs wide, straddling the smaller man's face. Elmo smiled and dove headfirst into Bear's fuzzy crack, forcing his tongue deep inside the snapper's hole. Bear grabbed a handful of Elmo's red hair and forced his face deeper and deeper into his ass, closing his eyes as the running back lapped and munched on his sensitive hole.

"Fuck me, dude. You know how to eat ass, that's for sure. Bet you been munching on a bud's a-hole for a long time. Shit, oh yeah, that's it, dude. Rim that furry fucker!" Bear moaned in pleasure as Elmo tongue fucked his anus in long wet strokes, reaching up to grip the man's huge penis as he did. "Shit, that feels so good. I need to piss, though, man. You either gotta let me pee or open up for some lemon Gatorade, dude."

Elmo pulled away from Bear's ass and knelt submissively in front of his large cock, mouth open and ready. Bear's eyebrows disappeared up into his bangs.

"You sure, man? You want this piss?"

"Feed me, sir," the small man said, gripping Bear's big round ass. The long snapper held his penis against Elmo's open lips and relaxed his bladder, sending a jet of straw-colored urine into his mouth. As it filled up his mouth, Elmo closed his mouth long enough to swallow, with the piss drenching his face and chest, before opening up for another long drink.

"Jesus, man. That is fucking hot. I always wondered about guys drinking piss. Holy crap, dude. This is so messed up," Bear said draining his bladder into the thirsty back's open mouth.

"I'll take your piss any time you want, sir. Yours and Dakota's too, if you want."

"Oh yeah? Well maybe we will tag team your ass one of these days. Suck my cock, now bitch," Bear ordered, sliding his erect penis into the man's mouth until he gagged. "Yeah, gag on that cock, runt. You been wanting my dick ever since you saw me get naked in the locker room. Yeah, I watched you stare at me and Dakota. You little cocksucker, you know some quality meat when you see it."

Elmo grabbed Bear's cock and wrapped his fist around the base and began to suck with gusto. He licked the shaft and head, he suckled the bull balls, then returned to his dick, swallowing as much of the thick tube as he could. Bear held the running back's ears and skull-fucked him deep and hard, his big balls swinging free and banging into the red-head's chin.

"Yeehaw, boy. Suck that dick. You are a class act cocksucker, dude," Bear said. The back's mouth was stretched wide, causing tears to leak from the corner of his eyes. "Shit, man. I am getting too close. Not yet. Get your ass up here," Bear ordered pulling Elmo up from the floor of the tub. "Assume the position, boy. Spread your little ass for me. Show me that pink pussy."

Elmo stood and spread his legs wide apart, reaching behind to pull his ass open. His pink rosebud was surrounded by a soft ring of copper fur. Bear dropped to a knee and inspected the anus, running his large finger around the lips.

"Holy fuck, that is a pretty pussy, Elmo." Bear's large finger invaded the tight muscle, causing the young man to groan and hold the wall with one hand. "Shit, I've never eaten ass before, but I am gonna munch on this," he said pressing his face and lips to the soft, puckered knot of flesh. He lapped and licked, forcing his big tongue inside the tight furry hole. "Goddamn, that's ten times better than the fishy pussies I've eaten," Bear said, his voice muffled in Elmo's muscular butt cheeks. Elmo held his hands against the wall of the shower and pushed his ass back into Bear's face, his eyes closed, almost catatonic.

"Okay, I am ready to fuck this pussy. Get your ass out of here and dry off. Get some lube in that tight hole, boy. And find me a condom, a big one!" Bear ordered. Elmo dashed out of the bathroom, drying off as he flitted around the room. Bear turned off the shower and methodically dried off, spending a long time shoving the towel up his ass and around his big balls. His cock was still rock hard, dripping a long string of precum on the Berber carpet. He walked into the bedroom and found Elmo on his bed, on his knees, his ass in the air wide open, with a large stream of lube running down his furry crack. There on the comforter lay a foil package for a Magnum condom. Bear opened the pack with this teeth and unrolled the rubber onto his fat cock, grabbing the lube and slathering it on his shaft.

"Fuck, that feels almost as good as fucking sometime. Okay, boy. This is gonna hurt," Bear said. Get your face down in that pillow. The long snapper held his penis against the juicy anus in front of him, tapping it and rubbing it against the furry crack. He wedged his erection into the tight pucker and pushed forward with one long, hard thrust that flattened Elmo to the mattress. The running back howled into the pillow as Bear's fat nine inches of beef slammed balls deep into the tight, hot hole. Bear was relentless, fucking deep and hard, his balls smacking into Elmo's ass, filling the room with wet squishing sounds.

"Oh God, you're killing me. Fuck, you're ripping me apart, Bear," Elmo groaned into the pillow.

"Keep that shit quiet, boy. You wanted to get fucked by a real man, now take it like one. Oh shit, here I cum!"

Bear pulled out of Elmo's ass and ripped off the condom. He held his cock and watched as a fire hose of semen sprayed a thick rope of seed in the running back's tight crack and against his wrecked, pulsing hole. Four, five, then six spurts of semen coated the redhead's ass. Bear used his hard penis to push a load of the nut into the running back's spent hole, sliding it deep inside, then pulling out, and shoving more seed into Elmo's ass.

"Jeezus, Elmo. I haven't cum that much in a long time. Had to breed you with that shit, shove a bunch of my nut into your pussy. You're probably pregnant now," Bear said flopping back on the bed. He pulled Elmo to him, wrapping his arms around the small man. "Jerk your dick off now, dude. I want to see you cum."

Elmo grabbed his penis and jacked it up and down for thirty seconds before a long white rope of cum splattered on the red belly fur covering his six pack. Bear scooped up some of the warm sperm and tasted it. "Nice tasting nut, bro. Shit, I think I am gonna sleep great. Okay, get the hell off me and go clean up again...and bring me a wet washcloth.

At 6:00 the next morning, Dakota opened his eyes. Connor still lay beside him. They had woken in the middle of the night and sucked each other off once again. His cock was hard now and he let it slide easily into the kicker's smooth ass crack, pushing against his hole. He pulled out and Connor magically produced a condom pack from somewhere and helped Dakota slide it on his rigid penis. The kicker moved his ass back and forth, feeling the lube from his precum ease the tip of his penis further and further into the opening of Connor's ass. The kicker woke and gripped his right leg under the knee and pulled it up and wide open. Dakota pushed and felt Connor's anus open, allowing his cock to slide deep within. The punter let his thrusts pull almost all the way out before plowing back against the Hawaiian's round ass. He reached around and grabbed the kicker's cock, stroking it as he fucked. He lasted less than a minute before unloading his nuts into the condom deep inside Connor's bowels. The man moaned, and warm semen flowed over Dakota's hand. Part of him instantly felt guilty. Did he just lose his virginity with Connor...or did it not count until Bear's huge cock slid inside his own virgin hole?

The guys silently moved into the bathroom and climbed in the shower together, washing each other off, feeling unusually shy and restrained. Dakota's mind was reeling, what the hell is going on, he thought. Connor stood behind him, his arms wrapped around the punter's belly, pulling him tight against him.

"Hey man," the kicker said in the spraying water. "Don't overthink this. You and I aren't going to be boyfriends or more. Shit, as far as I'm concerned, it was just mutual masturbation, with a little more spice. I'm not sorry, either. It was fucking hot and felt great. But it's just teammates having fun, burning off some energy and scratching an itch together." The solid Hawaiian player turned Dakota around to face him. Their dicks rubbed against one another. "It's probably none of my business, brah, but I think you might need to talk with Bear about your feelings, though. It's pretty obvious you boys are most definitely 'in like' with each other and I think it might be more than that. Me...I think I still like pussy enough to know this is just some fun on the side. But you gotta figure out if it's the same for you, or if maybe he just might be your 'kāne.'"

Dakota soaked in the words and the meaning, wrapping his arms around the kicker and kissing him on the side of his head. "I know you're right, bro. I've got some shit to figure out. And, yeah, that fucking was smoking hot, no matter whether you like puss or dick."

Connor smiled, letting his fingers slide up and down Dakota's crack, teasing his hole. "You gonna punt that ball like a mo-fo today, brah. Let's get out of here and get some food."

The guys dried off and dressed in sweats and grabbed their gear and started down to the banquet hall and breakfast. As they waited for the elevator with several other players, Bear showed up looking distracted and sheepish. Connor smiled and patted the big player on the shoulder.

"You okay there, big guy?" he asked.

"What? Oh, yeah. Just still sleepy. You seen Koda?"

"I'm right here," Dakota said from behind the big long snapper. Bear turned around, a mixture of happiness and worry on his face.

"Can I talk to you a second?" Bear said in sotto voce.

"Sure."

Bear looked around and saw the stairwell as the group of guys boarded the elevator. Bear nodded with his head toward the stairwell and Dakota followed him. Once inside, the big player dropped his bag, standing in front of Dakota, a pained expression on his face.

"I..I need to tell you," Bear started.

"Me too," Dakota answered.

"Um, things kind of got a little crazy last night. You know, between me and Elmo. I just…it was stupid and didn't mean anything but I woke up today feeling like shit and…"

Dakota laid a hand on the side of Bear's furry face. "Exactly the same for me, bro-seph. It was a crazy night for me and Connor too. Look…forget it. Doesn't matter. I don't care about him or Elmo or any of the other guys like you. You are my bud, my BF, my roomie…my brother.

So, fuck it, man. Let's just forget the night, chalk it up as a crazy ass wank session and go play some football and fuck up these stupid Loggers."

Bear's warm brown eyes welled up with tears, his hand grasping Dakota's on the side of his face. A big grin began to spread across his face. Bear's other hand held on to Dakota's face and he pulled the punter toward him, their nose and lips only a millimeter apart.

"You said just what I needed, bubba. Let's go balling. I love you, man," Bear whispered and his lips touched Dakota's. They were warm, almost hot and thick. His furry mustache and beard softly tickled Dakota's sparse mustache. The moment Bear's lips touched his, Dakota felt like electricity was coursing through his body, setting his nerves on fire. His dick instantly hardened and his heart sped up like he was jogging. Bear pushed him backward until his head and back were against the wall. Dakota felt Bear's huge cock press against his belly. Bear opened his mouth and Dakota's tongue slid inside, touching, tasting, teasing the big player. Their arms slid around one another and hugged so tight the punter thought his ribs would crack. They pulled apart, looking deeply into one another's eyes.

"I love you, Bear," Dakota said, allowing his lips to lightly kiss the man again.

"Holy shit, bro..," Bear whispered. His face lit up like Moses on the mountain. "I...I..."

"Shhhh," Dakota said. "Let's go fuck up some guys on the ball field."

"Sounds great, brother," Bear said sliding his arm around Dakota as the two picked up their bags and practically ran down the stairs to breakfast.

The game was a slaughterhouse. From the kickoff, which the Wolves returned for a touchdown, to forcing not one, but two safeties, to 55 yard field goals and punts dropped inside the five yard line, WOU butt raped the Puget Sound Loggers like they had never been whipped before. The football gods were clearly in love with the Wolf Pack today. The final score of 55-0 was bad enough, but the reality was far worse. The Wolf Pack demolished Puget Sound in every aspect of the game. The defense made two picks for touchdowns. They didn't allow the Loggers to make more than three first downs and PSU never made it past midfield. The offense was lights out, making every run and pass look effortless. And the special teams were, well...special. Dakota even got to slide up underneath Bear's big backside in the fourth quarter and hand off and pass the ball along with second stringers due to the game being so out of reach. Every movement, Dakota telegraphed to the snapper with his hands on the man's ballsack. It was like they shared a brain, which just happened to be connected through his scrotum!

In the showers after the game, the players jumped up and down and partied like it was 1999 as the music of Prince blasted on speakers. Dakota stopped counting how many players smacked his ass, gave him hugs, and even kissed the side of his face. Five or more of the players had given him the Chicago Cubs dick bump, mashing their naked cocks together. He wasn't completely sure but he thought that when QB Blake made his way through the steamy clouds in the shower to dick bump him, it seemed like the senior's hand gripped his ass and a soapy finger slid inside his hole right up to the knuckle. There was no doubt that when married tight end, Alex, hugged him, the man squeezed Dakota's half-hard dick with his hand and shouted 'Great game' to the freshman. Bear stood beside Dakota and the punter watched as Leon and other defensive linemen hugged the naked snapper, patting his large round ass or dick bumping him as well. Dakota smiled as Blake's finger disappeared into Bear's deep crack as he had with the punter, the expression on Bear's face priceless as the QB penetrated his tight hole. As the guys dried off beside their locker, Coach Kelly had walked by and patted both of them on their naked ass, congratulating them on a ball's out game. Dakota returned the pat, noticing that the coach's penis was clearly outlined in his thin shorts as he did.

The team continued to celebrate at a local restaurant after the game, the spirits of the younger players somewhat dampened by the inability to consume alcohol. The best part of the evening was a highlight video reel the athletic department showed the team on the big screen with all the best plays. There were cheers and hoots, guys pounding on Dakota's back when his punts landed inside the five or messing up Connor' s hair with this 55 yard field goal. The defensive line guys pounded on Bear when one of his tackles was shown, clearly knocking the Logger's D-Lineman over like a rubber doll as he charged forward, blasting the guy out of bounds nine yards away. Maybe the best moment, however, was a close up of Elmo and Dillon standing alongside each other on the bench. The last names on their jerseys filled the screen...FONDA COX. It took only two seconds for the team to explode in laughter. Elmo and Dillon tried to laugh off the teasing, but Dakota could see the scarlet flush in their cheeks.

The team boarded the bus around 8 PM for the long ride back home. The mood on the bus was loud and celebratory for the first hour, with plenty of high fives and even a few more dick bumps. But soon, the team had settled down in their seats, most with headphones on. The lights in the cabin were off and it was dark on the bus. The sound of snores could be heard pretty much everywhere, which made the headphones even more helpful. Elmo and Dillon had slumped into the seats across from Bear and Dakota, curled up underneath a blanket since the O-Linemen had gotten the driver to crank down the A/C to sub-arctic level. Dakota and Bear scooted down in their seats, leaning them back for a bit more room and comfort, covered up with a blanket as well. As the team settled down and night darkened the inside of the bus, Dakota slid his hand into Bear's big mitt that rested in his lap against the large bulge in his shorts. Dakota moved his fingers over the snapper's cock until he felt it swell against his touch, warm and hard, his pulse tapping against his touch. Bear reached down and slid the elastic of his shorts underneath his huge sack. Dakota's slid his head over onto Bear's shoulder and moved his hand to slowly fondle the egg-sized testicles soft and warm in the loose sack.

"I missed sleeping beside you last night," Bear whispered in the softest voice he could manage, right into Dakota's ear.

"Me too, buddy. Just wasn't the same."

"I still feel weird about...you know..."

Dakota squeezed Bear's cock, feeling it fill with blood against his palm. Bear's hand maneuvered into the punter's lap, sliding the loose leg of his shorts up and freeing his penis from his shorts. The tip was already leaking precum which Bear rubbed on his thumb and then quietly licked off before returning his hand to grip his roommate's pecker.

"Did you guys fuck?"

Bear stayed quiet for a bit, softly fondling Dakota until he was fully erect. "Yeah. What about you?"

"Yeah. I boned Connor. Didn't see that coming."

Bear chuckled. "Same for me. Elmo pulled out the Magnum and I fucked the shit out of his little hole."

Dakota snickered. For some reason, just hearing Bear say that made him feel better somehow. He slowly jacked the big man's cock up and down, feeling Bear's hairy leg press hard against his own. "So how was it?"

"Tight. Tighter than I expected since I think that cat is a fucking man-hoe."

Dakota laughed. "Connor is a kind and decent guy with a fucking hot ass for sure…but…"

"But what, bro?"

"Just didn't compared to how connected I feel to you."

"Ditto, honey," Bear said so softly it was barely audible. "The whole time I Was fucking that red furry hole, I was imagining it being you."

"Really?"

Bear slowly jacked Dakota's cock. "You know it, buddy. I don't know what the hell is going on with me."

"Me either, big guy. But I am loving it, whatever it is."

"You have no idea how that makes me feel to hear you say that," Bear said. "My Pops would lose his shit if he knew about this."

"What do you mean?"

"That I am fucking in love with you, Koda. I never knew I would feel like this with another guy. But I'm just gonna say it, brother. I love you. I think about you and your sweet ass all the time. And even thought I fucked that redhaired fuzz ball, I kept the condom on and he never touched my pussy. I saved that for you, man. I want to feel you inside me, bare, breeding me like a bull. I want to get so full of your fuckin' cream that it spills out all over the sheets. And I want to fuck you until your eyeballs roll back into your head like a slot machine."

Dakota looked at Bear, his eyes wide, mouth dry. He swallowed hard, squeezing the massive penis in his hand, feeling the precum leak onto his fingers. He moved his hand and slowly sucked the drips off his fingers, slowly sliding his fingers one at a time into his mouth.

"Oh my fuckin' God," Bear groaned.

"So you think you're still a virgin?"

Bear smiled slightly. "As far as I'm concerned...abso-fuckin-lutely."

"Good. Because I feel exactly the same. I want to bury my face in your hairy hole and suck your ass until you beg me to breed you. I want my cock to explode inside you and cum so much, you think it's a fuckin' enema."

"Dude...that is so nasty. And fuckin' hot, man. Shit, we are such gays right now."

"I don't care. Maybe my dad will freak, or maybe he already knows I like dick. Maybe that's why he gave me Tom Brady to fucking play with."

"Oh snap, bro. That's even hotter."

"And maybe your cowboy dad has ridden a couple of cocks himself out there on the range, fixing the fence with his friend."

"Shit man, I have actually wondered that before." Bear's penis flowed like a river of precum that Dakota continued to lick away.

"I want that monster cock of yours to pop my cherry so hard, everyone in the whole fucking world will know. I have no idea how you are gonna get that big guy up in my asshole, but it's gonna be so sweet working it out."

"Fuck, bro. You are killing me."

The players stroked and fondled each other more, their faces close enough to feel each other's breath. Bear raised his face up and looked across at the two on the other side of the aisle. Dillon's head was laying against the window. Elmo had slumped down far in the seat, with his head now under the blanket. In the dim light, you could just make out the slow bobbing up and down of his head under the fleece.

"Damn. Looks like we aren't the only gay cockgobblers on the team. That's fucking hot...and kinda dangerous," Bear whispered.

"You want me to blow you, bro? I will if you want."

"I would love it, but let's just wait til we get home. Cause there is no way I could be quiet on this bus when I shoot my nut in your hot mouth, sweetheart." Dakota squeezed the big dick in his hand causing Bear to softly moan. Dakota whispered.

"Have you ever felt like this before with another guy?"

"Nah. I mean, I've sorta had the hots for a ranch hand or boy in class before, but mostly just because I was so fuckin' horned up all the time anyway. But nope, I never felt like I was falling for a dude. You?"

"Never. I jacked off fantasizing I was fucking around with guys before. I mean, I already told you I look at gay porno all the time. I think my dad knew about that a lot which might be why he gave me Tom Brady." Bear laughed.

"I know I keep saying your toy is Brady...but really, all I think about is your tight furry hole when I am fucking that thing?"

"Same for me. And I have to tell you, man. I know we are around a ton of hot swingin' dicks all the time...which I do love gawking at. But at the end of the day, all I really want is to fuck you, bro." The guys squeezed each other's erections softly again, slowly jacking one another so the blanket didn't move too much. "I have to tell you, B...when you kissed me yesterday before the game...it was like a dream came true. I had wanted that from the first night we laid in our stupid beds together. No girl I ever kissed came close to making me dick explode like kissing you did."

"It's all I've been thinking about too, bro-ski. That...and seeing if I could get my whole fuckin' head up your twat." Dakota smiled and pushed his shoulder even closer into Bear's side. "I'm just gonna keep saying it, bubba. I fucking love you. I want to be a couple with you."

"I want to fucking marry you, dude," Dakota said. "How crazy is that?"

"I feel the same. I want to fucking have babies with you. Can't you just see us with two little boys?"

"What if we had girls?"

"Eh...maybe we need to make sure they are boys. Me and little girls, I am all thumbs, man."

"You would learn, bro. But yeah, little boys are great."

"What the fuck are we talking about, man? Do you really think we could be a couple of gay football players? I know stuff has changed, but it would be so hard."

"It's already hard," Dakota said gripping Bear's fat cock. "But let's just get used to the idea that we are gonna be boyfriends first...and if you don't mind at first—can we keep it just between us? I'm not embarrassed or ashamed or anything, but it's a big deal."

"I know. I can't see another way yet either. What if we start fucking and we get bored with it and want some pussy?"

Dakota closed his eyes. "I don't see that happening, my friend. I just don't want a girlfriend. If I am being really honest. I never did."

"Neither did I, not even when my fingers or tongue were inside the va-jay-jay."

"Yuck," Dakota said. "More than I could ever do."

8. Losing the V Card

The bus made it back to the campus a bit after 3:00 AM. The team groggily unloaded their gear, helping the equipment managers as much as they could before stumbling back to their dorms and apartments. Dakota and Bear walked into their room, dropped their duffles, and pulled one another into a big hug, groping each other's butts, nips, and balls as they kissed deep and long, their tongues sucking and licking each other. Bear's scruffy beard tickled the punters face as he nuzzled his ear and neck and sucked lightly on his tongue and lips. Dakota's hand slid inside Bear's shorts, fondling the snapper's hard-on, gripping his bull balls tight and moving under his sack to his furry hole. After a few minutes of sweaty make out fondling, Dakota pulled away and looked at his roommate.

"I want to fuck around so much, but I am so sleepy, bro."

"Oh shit. I am so glad you said that because I am about to fall over," Bear said grinning, ruffling the short blond curls on top of the punter's head.

"You want to lay down and either jerk off or use Tom Brady or..."

"How about we suck each other's cock and then sleep. And when we wake up, I'm punching my V card. We have the day off and I wouldn't mind spending most of it naked and covered in your nut."

Dakota smiled and pulled his shirt over his head, letting it lay on the floor. He pushed his shorts and underwear down and went into the bathroom to take a long piss before bed. The big furry long snapper stripped down and stood beside his roommate, reaching over to grasp Dakota's hard dick as he pissed. Dakota grabbed Bear's cock. It was hot and rigid and he smiled as he felt the jet of urine flow out and into the toilet in a loud, frothy blast.

"Sword fight, Bro," Bear said pressing his shoulder against Dakota's, crossing their streams in the john.

"I wish I wasn't so tired," Dakota said leaning his face toward Bear's feeling the man's soft lips kiss the side of his face.

"Me too, bro-seph. Come on, I want a protein shake in my belly before bed." Bear gripped his penis and shook off the last drips. He grabbed Dakota's ass and marched him toward the bed. They climbed up into Bear's side and wrapped their arms around each other, their dicks leaking and hard as they groped and kissed. Dakota's fingers slid down Bear's furry ass crack and eased inside his tight hole causing him to softly moan and return the favor, sliding his fat fingers knuckle-deep into the blond fuzzy hole.

"Oh shit," Dakota hissed under his breath. The guys jacked and masturbated one another as they kissed. Then, pushing his legs up toward Dakota's face, Bear straddled the punter's head, lowering his penis down into his roomie's open mouth.

"Holy God, that feels so good, buddy," Bear said. He gripped Dakota's penis and swallowed it until the shaft was buried in his mouth all the way to the punter's short, blond pubes.

The men sucked, gripping the base of each other's shaft, tasting the slick precum that poured form the piss slits in their cocks. Dakota's gag reflex kicked in several times as Bear pushed his cock deeper into his mouth, but soon, both men began an easy-going sucking rhythm. Dakota could feel the river of saliva from Bear's mouth pour down his shaft, across his big balls and into his crack as Bear devoured his penis like a starving wolf. The man buried three fingers into Dakota's asshole, tapping his prostate and sending him over the edge.

Dakota groaned loudly, maybe too loudly, and dug his heels into the mattress and sent a river of semen flowing into Bear's lapping mouth. Bear's massive cock swelled more as it plowed it's way deep into Dakota's stretched mouth. He growled and clinched his big ass cheeks together and exploded five large hot blasts of nut gravy into his best friend's slurping mouth. The cum leaked from the corners of his mouth and slid down almost to his ears as he swallowed the sperm that just kept spurting from the massive mushroom head.

The boys sucked and cleaned one another's penis until they were glistening with spit in the dim moonlight of the room. Bear leaned up and collapsed beside his buddy on the pillow, wrapping him in his big arms.

"Holy goddamn fucking shit…" Bear said.

"Exactly," Dakota whispered. They fell asleep in under a minute.

When Bear awoke in the morning, he smiled as the sensation of a hungry tongue buried deep in his asshole flowed over him. He reached around and grabbed his buddy's head and mashed his tongue further inside. He spread his legs wider, loving the sensation of Dakota's hungry munching on his furry hole. Dakota slid two fingers inside and pressed relentlessly against the big guy's prostate until he was writhing around on the bed in agony.

"Oh sweet Jesus, that is off the chart, bro. How the fuck did you learn to do that?"

"Xtube," came Dakota's muffled reply. Bear laughed and laid his head down on his arms, drinking in the passion and hunger of Dakota's salad tossing. "Fuck, dude. You are going to town down there. You want me to go clean up or anything?"

"I don't know. I'm kind of digging the sweaty musky dirty ass more than I ever imagined. And besides, I watched you clean out your pussy pretty good in the showers after the game."

"Yeah, but that was hours ago, man. Oh fuck, you are doing a number on my button down there." Dakota grinned and slid his tongue back inside Bear's tight, hairy hole until it poured with saliva. The long snapper continued to lay with his eyes closed, concentrating on the thick long tongue bathing his balls and hole. His eyes opened wide as a cool, slick liquid flowed into his crack. He turned his head around to see Dakota pouring a generous helping of lube into his crack, slathering it lavishly on his own cock.

"Oh damn. Am I about to be an ex-virgin?" Bear said turning his head even further. His own cock was about to snap off as he laid on it. The blond punter slid forward on his knees until his dick head touched Bear's sensitive anus.

"Yeah brother. It's time." Bear looked back around, his eyes stared as he saw Dakota with his phone poised on the tip of his cock resting on Bear's furry hole.

"You're gonna film it?" he said incredulously.

"Well, it's a pretty historic moment. And I thought you might want to watch it later."

"Oh shit, that is so fucking nasty. Yeah, man. Give it to me," Bear whispered through clinched teeth.

"I am not throwing away my shot…" Dakota sang the line from *Hamilton*, leaning forward, gripping the tip of his dick until the large wide head slipped inside the lubed fleshy muscle. Bear buried his face in the pillow, gripping the sheets with white knuckled anticipation.

As Dakota's cock penetrated the man's asshole, Bear's head pulled up, his mouth open in a wide silent cry of pain. Dakota pulled back slightly, then rocked in and out and in and out, feeling the tightness in Bear's sphincter relax and accept his penis. More and more slid inside until his balls rested on his best friend's crack. It was the tightest, hottest, wettest thing he had ever felt. When he clinched his ass cheeks making his cock swell, Bear groaned into the pillow and raised his big ass up to take even more of his buddy's penis.

"Oh shit. Oh fuck, man. Yeah. Mmmmm. Keep doing that. You are hitting something in there, bro. Oh yeah, fuck that shit. Pound me, man. Harder. Goddamn it, I said harder!"

Dakota's face was drenched in sweat as he slammed his thick cock balls deep into his best friend. His own testicles rolled and mashed against the man's ass as he felt his seed beginning to boil in his balls.

"Oh God...Jesus, I am gonna cummmmmm!"

Dakota slammed his dick once more even deeper within the furry crack and deposited a giant eruption of semen into Bear McLeod's manhole. He fired again and again, sending more and more jizz into the tight furry hole until it leaked out and ran down Bear's wide stretched crack. Dakota collapsed onto the man's back, feeling his penis pulse inside his friend.

"Oh my fucking God. You just popped my cherry, big time bro. I am a fully-fledged gay now. Shit, I can't believe how amazing that felt to be owned by you like that. Your fucking cock felt like it was a fucking telephone pole.

"My first time fucking anyone," the eighteen year old newly unvirgined punter said feeling his cock slowly slide from his best friend's stretched hole. "Jesus...why did I wait so long for that?"

Bear turned around and pulled Dakota into his arms. "Because you hadn't met me, bro. You had to be the one to take my ass cherry, man. Was the sweetest pain I ever felt in my life."

"Sorry if I hurt you."

"Oh shit, dude. I think a big cock in you're a-hole is supposed to fucking hurt a little, he said kissing Dakota deep, touching his tongue to the man in his arms. "Let me go wash off some of your jizz, bro cause my balls are about to explode to do some damage to that virgin boy puss of yours."

Dakota sat up looking wary. "Suddenly, I am a bit scared," he said.

"Get your ass in the shower, boy!" Bear barked, smacking Dakota hard on the butt. The punter yelped and climbed off the bed. His cock was still fat and dripping and his balls swung heavy between his legs. "Holy God, I am gonna wreck that bobbum of yours."

The roommates turned on the shower and squeezed inside. It was a tight fit, but rubbing bellies and butts together only made the cleanup more fun. Bear's soapy hand slid inside Dakota's asscrack and found his pussy and slid two fingers inside, causing the punter to groan.

"Fuck, dude. Your fingers are like giant sausages. Oh man..." Dakota complained as he stroked his friend's cock that was leaking precum like a dripping faucet. "Oh shit, I gotta taste some of that," Dakota said sinking to his knees, sliding all of Bear's eight inches of beer-can thick cock into his mouth, or as far as he could without barfing.

"Yeah, boy. Take that cock. Mmmm, yeah, lick Dad's pecker you little twink. Yeah, I know you been wanting my man bone up in your tight virgin pucker for a long time now."

Dakota almost started to laugh, but went with the role play. "Oh yeah, Dad. I love how big your cock gets when I touch it. I don't think there's any way I can take it up in my hole."

"Oh, you're gonna fucking take it, boy. And it's gonna fuckin' hurt," Bear said pulling Dakota back up and letting his thick thumb push inside Dakota's stunned anus.

"Oh shit. Take it easy, Bear," Dakota snapped. Bear gripped his mouth and chin in his large hand and shoved two fingers inside, temporarily gagging the punter and shutting him up.

"Shut the fuck up, boy. You have been peeking on me jacking off long enough. I know you are a gay and want a real man's dick in your tight pucker. I am gonna breed you like a bull!"

Dakota's eyes widened and his cock swelled fully hard again.

"See. What did I tell you? That big boy dick of yours is ready for me to pop that cherry of yours."

Dakota swallowed and talked with this mouth full of fingers. "Is it gonna hurt, Dad?"

"Oh hell yeah. You are going to be walking funny for a week after I mount your ass. I'm gonna grab you by the pussy just like our asshole President."

Dakota smiled and mumbled with the fingers still in his mouth. He reached up and stroked Bear's hard cock, soaping up his black nest of pubes and feeling the silky hard shaft slide through his fist making his own dick swell again. He pulled on Bear's scrotum until the big player groaned and gripped his penis and slapped Dakota in the face with the hard meat.

"Take it easy, boy. Dad's balls are sacred. They are what made you, you little prick. Get back to sucking that cock. Oh yeah, that's it...and the sack, yeah, bathe my balls with your tongue, boy."

Dakota's eyes watered from the thrust of Bear's penis in and out of his stretched mouth. The huge balls slapped against his face. He tried to put them in his mouth, but they were just too big. He slid a soapy finger inside Bear's anus as he sucked his cock.

"Dude, you have already been way too familiar with Dad's asshole today. My pucker is still smarting from that goddamn butt raping you gave me. Okay, fuck this shit, Koda." Bear pulled Dakota up to his feet. "Assume the position, boy," he commanded, turning the punter to the wall and kicking his feet wide apart so that his sack and dick hung loose between his strong, muscled legs. Bear knelt behind his friend and pulled the meaty round ass cheeks apart, exposing his blond furry hole. Bear pressed his nose to the sphincter and inhaled. It was wet, musky, and tangy. He slid his tongue out and against the knuckle of warm flesh, licking up and down until the boy's crack ran with saliva. His large hands gripped the buttocks and pulled them so far apart, a round O opened and Bear jammed his tongue as deep inside as he could get. Dakota groaned and held on tight to the slippery wall. Bear pulled on the punters sack and sausage hard until the blond player cried out in pain.

"Take it easy, Pop," he said through gritted teeth.

"Shut the fuck up, Boy," Bear said spitting into the open hole and sliding his thumb into the tight wetness.

"Oh holy God," Dakota said. "Fuck, it's too much, Bear."

Bear ignored the complaints and sent his forefinger into the orifice as well, causing Dakota's legs to almost buckle as he finger fucked the boy's virgin hole mercilessly. He thrust the digits in and out, rocking the boy's balls and dick until they smacked against his belly. He alternated between his fingers and tongue drilling Dakota's pucker until the punter was groaning and begging for relief.

"Oh Christ, Bear. Fuck, you are killing me. I'm gonna cum again if you don't…"

Bear's big hand smacked down hard on Dakota's ass causing the boy to yelp. "I thought I told you to shut the fuck up!" Dakota moaned and whimpered but stayed quiet as Bear continued to ravage his asshole with his fingers and tongue. Finally, the long snapper stood.

"Okay, boy. I think that puss is ready. Get the fuck out and dry off. Get on your belly on the bed and hold on for dear life. Dakota obeyed, stepping out of the shower and grabbing a towel. He dried his body, making sure every crease and fold was dry. He spread his ass and dried his crack and made sure his sack and cock were dry as well. He climbed back up toward the bed, but Bear caught him.

"Just get your chest down on the mattress, boy. Leave your ass off and legs on the floor. Spread 'em wide, son. Dad's about your breed your hole and pop that cherry." Bears voice was low, quiet, and menacing. Dakota laid his chest on the bed, stretching his hands out, his face on the sheets. He could feel Bear's hot, solid body move in behind him. Thick fingers grabbed his nutsack and pulled down, opening his anus again. He groaned. He felt the flow of the Gun Oil lube slide down his crack and get pushed inside his virgin rosebud, first one, then two, then three fingers until his ass was burning like fire. The lube eased and relaxed his ass muscles that had never been stretched farther than his own finger could do. When he felt the tip of Bear's penis press against his hole, Dakota began to panic.

"Go easy man. You are way too big for my….OH MY FUCKING GOD!!!" Dakota balled the sheet into his fists and felt Bear mash his face tight against the mattress as his horse cock opened his boyhole and forced the mighty mushroom head of his eight-incher into the opening before halting. Dakota screamed into the covers, his legs trembling, his asshole on fire.

"Settle down, bubba. I'm not gonna fucking butt rape you like you did me," the snapper whispered into his ear. Bear's big furry arms wrapped around Dakota's head, pulling his head up, his big palms clamped hard around his friends open mouth. "That's it, baby. That's it. Just a little at a time. Oh yeah. Fuck me, bro you are impossibly tight. My cock is in heaven already. MMMM, yeah that's it. Just a bit at a time." Bear used his other hand to squirt more lube onto his thick shaft as it slowly impaled Dakota. With every thrust forward, the punter's cornhole dilated a bit more, easing the thick cock forward. After almost two minutes, Bear's belly rested against his best friend's round ass. As he squeezed his ass together, his cock swelled, dilating Dakota's hole even more. The punter groaned, but now reached behind him to pull his ass open further. His muffled voice croaked.

"Wow in the fuck did you get that python up my shitter, bro?"

"Magic…and a lot of lube. " Bear's lips were right against his friend's ear. "Bubba, I just popped that cherry. Punched that V-Card and it feels un-fucking-believable. Dakota turned his head and the men kissed, their tongues deep in each other's mouth.

"Hold on, brother. Now the fun begins," Bear said as he slid his mammoth cock all the way out of the punter's stunned ass until the mushroom head only was left inside. The he forced it all the way inside again in one long slow thrust, mashing his bull balls into Dakota's butt. The punter howled.

"Oh God, oh my fucking ass. Jesus, you…you are gonna. Oh shit, that's it, bro. Oh fuck you are hitting something up there. Oh goddamn,

Bear...you big fucking amazing cunt...oh yeah. That's it. Fuck me, brother. BREED ME!!!"

Bear plowed his full eight inches inside his good friend until his big balls were slapping at Dakota's ass like a drummer. He rocked and pumped until they both were sweating, groaning, and sticky wet. The thick cock slid easily in and out of Dakota's wrecked hole now. Bear picked the boy up and shoved him onto the bed, laying his weight on top of him and driving his cock even further inside.

"Oh God. Fuck. Are you drilling for oil or something? Shit, I can't take much more!"

The agony fueled Bear's lust until he knew he wouldn't last much long. He pulled completely out of Dakota's asshole with a snap, the punter groaning in relief. He flipped him over and pushed his legs apart and up toward his head and let his penis settled into the quivering anus that was still too astonished to know what had just happened. He pressed forward and entered his friend until he was balls deep, pushing the boys' legs wide apart and fucking him hard and fast like a cheap whore. Dakota's eyes were wild, popping out of his head. He reached up and gripped Bear around his neck and pulled the furry face close. As their lips touched, Bear exploded. His semen blasted out in five thick rockets, filling up Dakota's asshole and leaking out the edges. Bear collapsed on top of his roommate, his chest heaving, with sweat running down his face. He could feel his heart beat along with Dakota's, his penis throbbing with each pulse. The fat cock remained deep within the punter's stretched hole, oozing out more and more nut butter into the ravaged anus.

Bear rolled to his side to keep from crushing Dakota's chest any more. He held his penis inside his friend until it finally slipped out with a soft plop, a gush of sperm leaking out as well. The young men held one another close, their faces pressed against each other until they slipped away into a deep sleep.

Dakota woke an hour later, Bear sucking on his cock with gusto. The punter gripped the big face in his crotch and wrapped his long legs around him, fucking into the snapper's mouth and grunting loudly as he unloaded his nuts into his friend's mouth. Bear sucked and swallowed ever drop of semen then climbed up and let the contents of his mouth slowly drain into Dakota's open mouth. Then the men kissed and tongued each other, sharing the semen like a fine delicacy. Bear fell over and lay on the pillow beside his roommate, Dakota slowly jacking Bear's hard cock.

"I can't fucking believe I just swallowed my own jizz from your mouth, bro. That is both sick and fucking hot all at the same time," Dakota said.

"True dat," the bearded freshman said. "Fuck, bro. We are cockgobbling gays for sure now."

"Holy shit. What are we gonna do, man?"

Bear leaned up, his head on his hand, with a big grin on his face. "I think we are gonna spend ever free minute trying to get each other pregnant or something. But I'm not sure it's gonna work."

Dakota laughed. "I'm serious, brother. What does this mean? I mean, are we gonna keep it quiet, are we gonna be a couple? Do we tell our dads? I am freaking out a bit."

Bear pulled Dakota into a hug. "Hey…hey…hey. Bubba, take a breath. I don't know what we are gonna do about all that yet. We are college freshmen football players, so it's a bit different for us, even though It shouldn't be. One day at a time, okay? As long as at the end of the day my dick is in your mouth or ass or yours is in mine, then it's all good. We will figure it out. My dad will kick my ass, but fuck that, cause I don't care. Maybe in time, we can pull a Michael Sam and come out to the team, but we don't have to do that either. But goddamn it, bubba, I am fucking in love with you. Fucking you like that…I didn't think sex could be that hot. We traded those V Cards pretty damn good though, don't you think."

"Best cherry pop ever, bro-seph. Way better than fucking Connor, even though he's got a nice ass."

Your fucking hole was so tight, man. Elmo…he was like an old used slinky or something. Glad I gloved up with him."

"Let's not talk about those guys right now. I don't like thinking of your perfect cock in Elmo's furry red hole."

"Deal – nor yours in Mr. Mahalo's cornhole. Though I am a bit curious. Maybe I'll tap that Hawaiian hole myself."

Dakota climbed up on top of his best friend. "You better fucking not," he said grinning. "Unless we can pump his poi together."

"Sounds like a plan. You hungry, brother?"

"Fuck yeah. I could eat the ass out of a long snapper. Oh wait, I already did that!"

Bear roared and kissed Dakota deep and long, rubbing his hard cock against the punter's belly.

TO BE CONTINUED...

Special Teams: Sophomore Year Sucks

Printed in Great Britain
by Amazon

69349782R00066